Also by Jonathan Strong
TIKE *And Five Stories*

OURSELVES

OURSELVES

a novel by Jonathan Strong

An Atlantic Monthly Press Book

Little, Brown and Company

Boston — Toronto

LIBRARY OF CONGRESS CATALOG CARD NO. 73-152907

T07/71

SECOND PRINTING

An earlier version of Chapter One was published in *Tri-Quarterly*.

ATLANTIC–LITTLE, BROWN BOOKS
ARE PUBLISHED BY
LITTLE, BROWN AND COMPANY
IN ASSOCIATION WITH
THE ATLANTIC MONTHLY PRESS

Published simultaneously in Canada
by Little, Brown & Company (Canada) Limited

PRINTED IN THE UNITED STATES OF AMERICA

for my parents

OURSELVES

~~~ 1 ~~~

J EFF KIMBERK and I were both
born on Groundhog Day, 1945, and that coincidence
was what first made us take note of each other seventeen
and a half years later. It was the day of my arrival at
Harvard College. Some fool was stopping everyone in
the stairwell of the dormitory and asking him when he
was born as a test of some esoteric theory of probabil-
ity. Jeff was bounding down two steps at a time as I
was struggling up with my steamer trunk which I rested
on the banister when the fool asked his question. "February second," Jeff and I replied in the same breath
and then looked at each other in amazement. Not that
we became friends at that point. My impression then
and throughout freshman year was that he did not wish
to be publicly associated with me on any grounds in

anyone's mind. Such paranoid impressions tormented me considerably in those days.

My birthday was the source of my college nickname, the Groundhog. That no one thought of applying it equally to Jeff bothered me, though I knew why well enough. He and all the others took to greeting me with, "How much ground would a groundhog hog if a groundhog could hog ground?" To which I was expected to reply, "A groundhog would hog all the ground he could hog if a groundhog could hog ground," not that I ever did. I would as soon forget those days and have no intention of referring to them further except when it might add the proper shading to this story of more comradely times. I had a long and bad late-adolescence, but it is over. Jeff and I are now old friends.

We lived in the same house as sophomores, but in different entries, and Jeff took a year in Europe after his junior year. When he returned, our original class had graduated, and he was surprised to find himself assigned to room with me. I had fallen behind too, though somewhat less voluntarily.

I had changed considerably by then. Our old classmates were no longer there to perpetuate my groundhog image, and Jeff could approach the situation anew. For one thing I was no longer the baggy and drab sort I had been when I was known as the Groundhog. My curly black hair had been allowed to grow. I let my fea-

4

tures and my hands express themselves — no more timid eyes, serious mouth, paws in pockets. I wore clothes which fit my shape, and instead of the old grays and browns, I wore whatever cheerful colors I felt like.

Jeff did not even recognize me at first. When he looked closer he said, "Oh, it's you," but there was an edge of pleasant surprise in his voice. He called me Xavy from the start and only referred to the ground-hog business when the second of February came around. I suppose he did not want to feel he had a groundhog for a roommate and probably feared someone else might dig up the old nickname to embarrass him.

Jeff was considerably taller than I was and had much lighter and straighter hair which he, too, soon ceased to have cut. His eyes were blue, his features sharp. My Portuguese blood showed in my rounder features, my black eyes, and of course my almost African hair, once the curse of my life.

Jeff's body was naturally sure of itself in a way that mine, however I might liberate it, would never be. I never saw him drop anything or miss catching something, while I was as likely to drop a ball as catch it. He never tripped up or stubbed his toes, but I was always a stumbler, and my ankles sometimes simply buckled under me. I do not know why. It may have been a symptom of my timidity.

We graduated together, though there was some question whether I would make it. My year off had cured me of bookwormishness, and I only managed to finish three late term papers the day before graduation. Jeff and I had decided to continue rooming together after college, but in a share-and-share-alike fashion with whoever else might need a place to sleep. I was glad to have a circle of friends at last and particularly one good friend to depend on. The problem of the draft had been solved for both of us by Jeff's allergies and my psychiatric difficulties. I found a job at a bookstore, and Jeff had a trust fund.

Neither of us felt under any pressure to plan out a course of life. Our original classmates were in medical schools and law schools or in the army, but we were just doing a little more thinking, a little waiting. We rejected the idea that twenty-two-year-olds must at once begin their future careers, but I admit we were awfully uncontributory, unwilling to dedicate ourselves to anything, and quite presumptuous of our rights and privileges. I suppose I still am.

We rented the ground floor of one of those gray frame buildings which line up one after another in Somerville, a town with lower rents than the famous two-university town next to it. Somerville was much like the town I grew up in, and I felt at home there. Our furniture consisted of a card table, two dustbag armchairs, and several bare mattresses. Needless to say it was a temporary arrangement, and we found a more civilized place in September. That was after Susannah

Twombley had made her appearance, but before I bring in Susannah, let me establish Jeff and me by ourselves.

Scene: Beethoven piano sonatas dropping one by one on the automatic stereo, the ceiling globe surrounded by light green bugs, the windows open and the yellowed shades flapping in the light breeze; a very sticky summer evening. Jeff in a pair of madras bermudas, leftovers from his sharp collegiate wardrobe, reading The Good Soldier *in the maroon armchair; Xavy in torn-off Levi's on one of the mattresses reading* Victories in Defeats.

Jeff: We should buy a fan, you know.

Xavy: You buy it. You've got the cash.

Jeff: I think I will.

Xavy: Good.

Jeff: It goes in my room, though.

Xavy: Fair enough.

Jeff: Of course I know it'll end up out here most of the time.

Xavy: I won't touch it.

Jeff: I wonder if I should get an exhaust fan or a rotating one.

Xavy: Suit yourself.

Jeff: Exhaust fans never seem to do anything.

Xavy: It's all in your mind.

Jeff: (*After quite a pause*) I think I'll get a rotating fan.

Xavy: Good.

Jeff: Tomorrow. (*They return to their books.*)

Scene: Jeff's room, bright sunlight outside, a fan rotating on the windowsill blowing on Jeff asleep in his underwear on a sheetless mattress, the torn windowshade pulled down to the top of the fan. A very fluffy brown and white cat walks across Jeff's back and wakes him up.

Jeff: (*Yelling*) Xavy, get your fucking cat out of here.

Xavy: (*From the hall*) It's not *my* fucking cat.

Jeff: Get it out anyway.

Xavy: (*Enters, in jeans, T-shirt, sandals*) Come on, Aztec. Hey, Az! It's time to get up anyway. Come on, Aztec.

Jeff: No it isn't. What time is it?

Xavy: Eight thirty. I'm going to work.

Jeff: Good night. (*Xavy departs with the cat under his arm.*) Shut the door. I don't want that fucking cat in here again. (*Xavy slams the door; Jeff yawns.*) Oh boy.

Scene: a summer storm, late Saturday afternoon, Bruckner's Sixth at full volume, the windows wide open, shades up, water pouring straight down. Xavy and Aztec in the navy blue armchair, the former reading Fathers and Sons; *Jeff and a girl named Elly in the kitchenette making fudge; four anonymous legs visible*

8

through the double door on a mattress in Xavy's room.

Elly: Get your fingers out of the fudge!

Jeff: Yes, ma'am.

Elly: Hand me that spoon.

Jeff: Yes, *ma'am!* (*Pause, some giggling.*)

Elly: Cut it out, Jeff.

Xavy: (*To Aztec*) Like the rain, Az?

Jeff: (*Coming into the living room*) I'm not very co-operative. (*Pause.*) Couldn't you put on something else, Xavy?

Xavy: What's wrong with this?

Jeff: You always overdo things. You've been playing Bruckner's Sixth at full volume all week. The neighbors must know it by heart.

Xavy: I just bought it.

Jeff: But you don't savor things, Fereira. You run them into the ground.

Xavy: Why is everyone so picky? Elly's picky, you're picky. (*Jeff sits in the maroon armchair, stretches, and stares out the window.*)

Jeff: Sure is coming down.

These scenes remind me of the way it was, not that anything particular happens in them. I really could not reconstruct the more important scenes of that summer, such as the huge fight we had after Jeff ran over Aztec (it had been my sister Susie's cat that I was keeping for the summer) or the long conversation in which Jeff told me all the details of his first true love affair in Europe during his year off. Those scenes would probably tell more about our friendship, but they have not stuck in my mind. I remember the reading of books, the listening to records, the dumb conversations. It was part of the thinking and waiting we were doing. And it surprised me that Jeff seemed at times as much at a loss as I.

I come from a large family. Besides my sister Susie two years younger, I have an older married brother Mike, a younger brother Tony, and a sister Lucy who is still in high school. I come from this part of the country, a mill town with a fair-sized Portuguese community. My parents are rather well off by local standards. I went to a second-string prep school on a partial scholarship and then amazed everyone by getting into Harvard. My parents had always suspected I had it in me but had never been quite sure and had not got their hopes up. Neither of them had ever gone to college.

Jeff is a midwesterner and as Anglo-Saxon as they come. He has one sister, Zada, now a sophomore at Radcliffe. Even every one of his grandparents had a college degree, and there are two colonial governors in his genealogy. However, he did not go to a prep school. The Kimberks lived in one of those self-sufficient suburbs with an unexcelled public school system.

The differences between Jeff and me did not affect our friendship, at least not in any profound way. The times he came up for dinner, Jeff tried to feel at home with my family and to admire it in its way, and I was

10

careful not to seem intimidated by such things as the box at Orchestra Hall when I visited Chicago.

But back when we were freshmen, before we really knew each other, Jeff Kimberk produced two strong reactions in me. Publicly I considered him an unimaginative cool snot and disliked him, while in my private fantasies I forgave him the groundhog business and imagined wishfully that the things I did not like about him, the snotty things, were simply defensive reactions, that underneath he was as uncertain as anyone else and that we could somehow become friends.

By sophomore year that fantasy faded. I did not see much of Jeff anyway, and I tried to write him off as an unfriendly person to whom I had been attracted in an insecure adolescent way. But my freshman fantasy later proved close to the truth. Jeff had indeed been on the defensive. He never had anything against me at all and had simply been playing along with the power structure.

Consider the effect of finding I could be friends with him. If someone seems initially desirable to know there will always be a kind of prize waiting for you when you feel at last you have secured his friendship. What I wish to say is that rooming with Jeff did enough for my self-esteem to allow me to jump almost immediately into a new way of thinking about myself.

Susannah Twombley came from Huntington, West Virginia. She appeared in the midst of a crowd of six or seven peripheral acquaintances of ours who needed a place to stay over Labor Day weekend. She had been studying piano in New York City and was now looking for a job as a piano teacher in Boston.

She made quite an impression on each of us. She was quiet, unlike Jeff's Elly, and simply sat amid the crowd and was serenely beautiful. Her long red hair, her green eyes, her sunburn, her long pianist's fingers: it is hard to put them all into a portrait. Certainly the contrast of red hair and green eyes struck us most. I remember her leaning against the wall, elbow on knee Hindu-style, her head tilted slightly, her bright green eyes looking up at the peeling ceiling. The orange and brown dress she wore, made from one of those Indian bedspreads, left only her hands and face uncovered. By Monday each of us knew her expressions and gestures very well because neither of us could stop watching her.

She thumbed through our records, scanned the titles of our books which stood about in piles, helped in the kitchen, and slept on the floor at the side of a fat girl named Betsy and Betsy's sweaty, bristly boyfriend. Jeff was still sleeping with Elly though they were fast falling apart, and I was casually involved with an unattractive girl named Bonnie who needed no seducing to speak of. I was in my experimental stage, making up for lost time. I am sure that is why when the time came it was Jeff Susannah fell in love with and not me.

As Jeff has explained it since, one thought tormented him all weekend: that this Susannah was the most perfect girl he had yet encountered, but as fate had it he

12

was still ridiculously messed up with Elly and would miss his only chance for her. He could not hope that Susannah would ever cross his path again. The memory of her would be all that would remain to torment him. I told him he was jumping to too many conclusions.

My own feelings were quite different and, frankly, acquisitive. Susannah was the most desirable person there. I had fallen back on Bonnie because she was so easy, but I was determined to make the effort of pursuing Susannah even though it was unlikely she would be interested in me.

The caravan of uninvited guests disbanded after Labor Day. Susannah moved in with a girl friend on Beacon Hill, and I got her phone number from Betsy who was the last to leave.

Jeff and I spent the week moving and arguing over what to buy for our new place, a fourth-floor flat overlooking a gas station. He wanted to get a lot of cheap, used things; I only wanted things I might want to keep. Consequently my bedroom ended up with one beautiful brass bed in it and that was all, while his had a mattress, a rickety dresser, an old office desk, a wicker chair, a frayed oriental rug, a grotesque standing lamp, and ratty curtains from Goodwill Industries. I compensated by painting the floor of my room black, the walls Chinese red, and the woodwork and ceiling gold. It took several weeks, and I was rather proud of the results.

I gave Jeff free rein in the living room because he got such a charge out of buying tacky things. The kitchen and bathroom were unredeemable, so we simply avoided spending time in them. Jeff got a job working as a research assistant to some sociologist, and I stayed on at the bookstore and then quit and started doing nothing again. That was after he and Susannah had fallen in love.

When I first phoned Susannah she had just found a job as a music teacher at a special school in Roxbury. She was so pleased and excited that she did a lot of talking for the first time. I am ashamed to admit, but I must admit, that I paid little attention to what she had to say. The prime motivation in all my calls to attractive girls had always been the expectation that I might get something out of them. I would work up my nerve for the call by thinking of one thing only, and all the time I was talking it was the only thing I was really thinking of.

Dr. Lichty, my psychiatrist, is good at catching me on the use of words. For instance, when I talk about Jeff's sexual activity I use the phrase, "He was sleeping with," whereas when I speak of my own I say, "I had sex with." I would never have noticed it, but Lichty says I invariably make the distinction, giving Jeff's behavior a certain quality of sentiment but characterizing my own as mechanical. I have great doubts about my capacity for tenderness and the generosity of my approaches to people.

And yet something about Jeff strikes me as selfish too. I had better say more about it before I get to that

14

unfortunate night in late September when I invited Susannah over for dinner. Jeff is selfish in a way I am not. I am selfish out of a lack of self-confidence, selfish in my attempt to pile up enough esteem to feel sufficiently safe giving back. This is a psychological problem, one I am honestly tackling in therapy, and, as unpleasant as my behavior may still be at times, I am ashamed of it and am desperately trying to do something about it. I am not the sort who at age twenty-four watches helplessly as his behavior patterns set into a mold. I truly do desire to learn greater humanity and find a satisfaction in my own spirit which will allow others to admire me.

But Jeff's selfishness is quite different and likely to increase with age. His cautiousness with new people and his possessiveness indicate a conservative nature. Even when limiting his possessions, as he has recently, he holds on tightly to what he chooses to keep. Jeff was never the casual sharing sort. He had been quite uncomfortable in our summer place (though he denied it) and was anxious to get entirely set up all at once in the new one. He determined how much he could spend, and before I had even found my brass bed he had everything he needed all in its proper place. He would not even begin to look for a job until everything was organized.

It was a natural nest-building instinct, and I should not criticize Jeff for wanting to be complete and cozy. But when Dr. Lichty asked me how I truly felt about it, I had to reply, "I felt it was silly to get so holed up, so sure of yourself, not to want to be freer. What sort of life will you lead at fifty if at twenty-two you set yourself down behind a little door with all your things about you?" And Lichty said, "Then that was how you felt about it. Don't apologize for it."

Dr. Lichty has been willing to extend his approval to things he knows I must grow out of because he knows it is the approval I am after and once I have it I am likely to say, "Hey, wait a minute, maybe I would like to settle down a little after all." It has taken some daring for him to do that. Jeff had the daring too. He always said, "If that's the way you feel about it, Xavy, then it's all right."

Jeff came home from work one night and found Susannah in the kitchen with me making dinner. He had not known she was coming. I had not even told him I had her number, and he was very surprised to see her. Immediately he dropped into a quiet mood and disappeared into his room.

Jeff's moods showed in his face rather obviously. When he was happy, his blue eyes brightened and his mouth got tense and ready to speak. When he was low, his eyes went dull, his lips drooped, and he got asthmatic. The awful noises Jeff would make having an attack truly frightened me. I had seen one of his worst ones after a game of soccer in the cold rain. His whole face swelled in awful puckers, and he threw himself around the locker room gasping for breath. It was called urticaria. He had been in the hospital with it three times already with oxygen tents and intravenous feedings, and the first time he actually might have died if the doctors had not got there in time to shoot him full of adrenalin. But it kept him out of the army, and otherwise he was in good shape. I always envied his athleticness.

Susannah looked at me as if to say, "What's wrong with him?" She was wearing one of her Indian dresses, but this one was not much more than hip length. Her sunburned arms were bare to the elbow, and she was long-legged and barefoot, in every way the kind of girl I most like to be with: quiet, soft, elongated, graceful.

I was wearing paint-stained jeans and a T-shirt. I would say that I am compactly built, but I am no outstanding specimen. My shoulders are rounder than Jeff's and not nearly as broad, and though I am basically firm I am not what you would call muscular. My skin is much darker than Jeff's, and my face, unlike his, does not reflect my moods. I am told I always look mild and calm.

We were cooking hamburg mixed with onions and mushrooms, sour cream, and soy sauce, improvising the proportions, doing a lot of tasting, and meanwhile setting the table in the living room. The kitchen was pale green, gray, or blue (I do not remember which). It had one filthy window high on a wall, cracks and peels everywhere, a grimy linoleum floor, and several sticky jelly jars in random places. The living room, on the other hand, had just been redone in Kimberk style, something

17

between 1930 Goodwill Industries and 1967 Bargain Basement: sagging couch, wobbly table, various uncomfortable plastic chairs. A red barrel stood in one corner with a few scraggly cattails sticking out of it, and mouldy junk-shop portraits of Shakespeare and Beethoven hung on the maroon-papered walls.

I do not recall what Susannah and I talked about. We probably filled each other in on our past lives or possibly talked politics, not a favorite subject of mine. At dinner with Jeff we talked about music. Jeff and I both loved music, and he loved it even more than books. It once surprised me that a sharp collegiate type could have such a feeling for it. He could hardly carry a tune himself.

We approached music in different ways. It was something relatively new for me, and so I used to get very excited when I discovered a new record and would play it and play it. But Jeff had been going to concerts since he was six and might decide he wanted to hear the "Waldstein" sonata, then some Vaughan Williams, then the Alto Rhapsody — some such mixed program, and never the same piece twice in a day.

Luckily our tastes coincided: beginning with Mozart, ending with Richard Strauss, allowing for Bach and Berg on each end — in general the great romantic tradition. But we used to have slight disagreements about performers. Jeff is an all-out romantic; I am more of a classicist. He loved Bruno Walter and Backhaus; I preferred Gieseking and Karl Böhm. Kathleen

18

Ferrier was his favorite singer; Victoria de los Angeles was mine.

That night Jeff chose Brazilian folk songs for dinner music. It was a record of mine left over from my prep school days when I had spent much of my time alone in my room privately studying the Portuguese world. Jeff had never played the record before. Perhaps he was trying to please me and keep himself in the background. I knew he was still tormented over Susannah. It was a Jeff-like feeling I was well acquainted with, and it was mean of me not to have warned him she was coming over.

Jeff was the sort who always seemed on top of things, but there were certain things, particularly matters of romance, which had a mystical quality for him. I have tried to be, for the last three years at least, reasonably at ease about sex, but Jeff always felt there was an uncontrollable pattern which he would either fit into or not. He thought Susannah had not been designated for him and that was that, while I tended to see the whole thing as a free-for-all for which it was merely a question of working up my nerve.

As we ate our hamburg and drank our Mateus, Jeff found himself talking despite his low mood. He said he had not known Susannah was still in town. She told him about her new job in Roxbury and her apartment on Beacon Hill. She spoke quietly, in short phrases, and with a distinctly Appalachian accent which Jeff and I found very appealing. I do not think of her accent any-

more (perhaps it has worn off a bit), but at the time
we noticed it most of all and liked it. I myself had gone
through a self-critical period when I upgraded my New
England accent from the raspy flat As of my hometown to the soft broad As of my prep school. It had surprised my parents, half pleased, half annoyed them,
but we never discussed it. Jeff, of course, had no re-
gional accent at all.

Susannah talked about her roommate, Ida Lee Sims,
who was from Huntington too and also taught in Roxbury. Jeff asked her how she liked Boston, and she simply said it was good to get away from New York. She
had considered going back to Huntington, but she felt
that would be giving up on her career. It seemed she
had high hopes for her piano playing.

She asked what the record was, and we got into a
discussion of the Portuguese language. I tried to teach
them to say the nasal *ão* sound. Jeff acted as if I had
just stepped off the boat (he liked the idea of being
best friends with someone of exotic extraction), and I
had to explain that only two of my grandparents had
actually been born in Portugal, and they had died before I was old enough to know them. Susannah wanted
to know if I spoke the language fluently, and I said I
had studied it on my own in one of my lonely root-seek-
ing periods at prep school but had forgotten most of it.
My parents had not spoken it since they were children.

Susannah had thought Xavier Fereira was a Span-
ish name. I explained there were a lot of Portuguese in

20

New England, it being directly across the ocean from Portugal, and I suggested we take a drive up the coast some day to see one of the fishing fleets if Jeff would loan me his car.

With the conversation back to me, Jeff was quiet again. I do not think Susannah felt the tension, but I knew a little contest was on and it was being judged by the topics we discussed. As long as we were on Portugal, Jeff felt peripheral. He let feelings of doom descend on him. But finally his natural friendliness and politeness got the better of his romantic mysticism, and he found a way back in.

"We never really talked," he said, "when you were here over Labor Day, about your piano playing, Susannah."

I remember her turning in her chair to face him. She had been looking across the table at me, but I saw her now in profile, the gentle line of her nose, her chin, and her neck pink with sunburn.

"I wish we had a piano here," said Jeff. "You know, Xavy, I almost picked one up for fifty bucks, but it would've cost as much to have it moved. What pieces are you working on now, Susannah?"

"I'm making an attempt on Schubert's B-flat sonata," she said.

"Oh, I wish we had a piano!" Jeff was excited, and his low mood faded out quickly. It was one of the mystical moments he believed in because the Schubert sonata was one of his favorites. I should have sensed the whole thing was up for me then and there.

"Then a Brahms intermezzo," said Susannah, "the Schumann *Symphonic Etudes*, Beethoven's Opus 90, the *Tombeau de Couperin*."

"All my favorite things," said Jeff. "We should go somewhere tonight where there's a piano. Xavy, do you suppose the Music Building's open?"

"Oh, I'll play for you soon enough," said Susannah. "There's plenty of time. I'm out of practice this summer. You know? I worked most of that up for my juries in May."

"But Susannah," said Jeff with a delighted smile, "am I ever glad to know someone who can really play!"

Why did I not give it up right then? It was so obvious they suited each other. Jeff leaned back in his chair, and his lips stretched out across his face in a grin. I had seldom seen him so overjoyed. Susannah cautioned him to wait till he heard her play to make up his mind about her talents, but that did not deflate Jeff's enthusiasm a bit.

I announced the dessert, Royal Anne cherries. Jeff said he was going to have a Twinkie instead. That got us into a discussion of his tacky taste, and I must have taken the opportunity to tear him down a little. But I think Jeff's unpretentiousness appealed to Susannah. He never tried to impress a girl, though he easily could have. It was part of his feeling that a romance would begin or it would not. Still there were times I felt he ate Twinkies a little too self-consciously, as though he were trying to get my goat. At other times I honestly believed he preferred them to Royal Anne cherries.

As soon as we finished doing the dishes, Jeff took me aside and said he would go out and leave me with Susannah. He was acting according to form, but I am sure it was only the doomed side of him that made the offer while the mystical side expected me to say, "No, Jeff, stay here, we're having such a good time, all three of us — I'm not trying to put the make on her anyway." I said no such thing of course, despicable sort that I was.

What I did say was, "Okay, Jeff, but I don't want to screw up your schedule."

"You did the same for me with Elly," he said. "I've got some research I should do at the library anyway. Back at midnight."

He left before Susannah came out of the bathroom. She seemed disappointed when I said Jeff had gone out, but the romance I sensed beginning between them may have been entirely imagined, a sign of my old paranoia.

Can I go on with this? It is going to be painful. When I have told it all I am going to take a day off from this writing, this self-discipline, and see what I can scrounge up in the way of a female. And then I will come back and start Chapter Two. With that end in sight, I continue.

Susannah and I sat on the fuzzy gray couch in the living room and listened to Backhaus play the first

Brahms concerto, her choice, and de los Angeles and
Fischer-Dieskau sing duets, mine. The duets did the
trick. Her head was on my shoulder. A duet by Purcell:

> *Lost is my quiet forever,*
>   *lost is life's happiest part;*
> *lost all my tender endeavours*
>   *to touch an insensible heart.*

One by Johann Christian Bach:

> *Ah, lamenta, oh bella Irene,*
>   *che giurasti a me costanza?*
> *Ah, ritorna, amato bene,*
>   *al primo amor.*
> *Qual conforto, oh Dio, m'avanza,*
>   *chi sarà la mia speranza?*
> *Per chi viver più degg'io*
>   *se più mio non è quel cor?*

One of Beethoven's Irish songs:

> *He promised me at parting*
>   *to meet me at the springtime here;*
> *yet see you roses blooming,*
>   *the blossoms how they disappear.*
> *Return, my dearest Dermot!*
>   *or sure the spring will soon be o'er.*
> *Fair long have blown the breezes,*
>   *oh, when shall I see thee more?*

I got up to turn over the record. When I sat down
again, closer to her, her hand crept around my waist
and my hand fell on her thigh. Schubert:

> *Nur wer die Sehnsucht kennt,*
> *weiss was ich leide.*
> *Allein und abgetrennt*
> *von aller Freude . . .*

People have been making love to these songs for a century or two (a nice thought). Why was she so ready to let me? It makes me angry to think about it now. On the other hand there is no sense laying the blame elsewhere, cowardly bastard that I am. "But how do you feel about it?" Dr. Lichty would say at this point. I happen to feel that part of the blame lies with me, but God dammit, part of the blame lies with her. I really had not expected her to respond at all and certainly not as readily as she did.

Susannah was a quiet girl, but she was also sensual. Just as I was excited by her body, she must have been excited by mine. I was not accustomed to such a quick response from a girl, and I still am not. It has always been a struggle for me, even with the least attractive ones, but this one time when I expected the greatest resistance I met none at all. It was quite a surprise, and I wondered how I had ever become so suddenly successful. At that time I still had many doubts about my attractiveness even though I was not as runty as I used to be and my curly hair had come into style.

We forgot the record and soon were tumbling around on the fuzzy couch. Susannah was limber and excitable, and we wrapped ourselves in various complicated positions. By the time side two was over and the automatic

25

stereo had shut itself off, Susannah's Indian dress was all but removed, the left sleeve having got tangled. To ease matters we went into my room with its smell of fresh paint. We finished undressing, and we made love by the light of the gas station next door because there were no shades.

I have never felt quite so exuberant in bed. I remember looking around to see her flat-topped knees clasping me in the pale light and then down at her hair spread on the pillow. Those images stick with me. Her sunburn was hot and tender, but she did not hold back at all. We said nothing the whole time except each other's names. There were moments when I felt I might fall in love with her, and those moments were the finest, the most abandoned.

At midnight we heard Jeff's key in the front door, heard him pad quietly in, and heard his door shut. Somewhat later we heard his door open, heard the toilet flush and his door shut again.

Susannah and I lay peacefully propped up on pillows, she nestling on my chest, my arms around her. Her long fingers still stroked the inside of my thighs, and I played with her breasts. It was the last pleasant moment of the evening. The gas station lights had been turned off, and now the full moon was in the window.

"Xavy," said Susannah.

"What?"

"I do like you." She was being careful and truthful.

"I like you too, Susannah."

"You do," she said. It was not a question. She was repeating the fact.

I could not find anything to say in return.

"I liked your lovemaking very much," she said. "You're awfully . . ."

"I'm awfully what?"

"I think you're . . ." She was quiet. I was running a finger softly over her face. I touched just under her eyes, and it was wet.

"Are you crying, Susannah?"

"A little."

"What is it?"

She was quiet, and I thought it best to lie quietly beside her and let her gather up what she was upset over, but I should have said something. Several months later when the awkwardness had been forgotten, a more explicit Susannah and a more responsive Xavy drank tea on a winter afternoon and talked over the time they had tried to sleep together and thought they understood their reasons for doing what they had done.

In the silence I must have dozed. Suddenly I sensed Susannah getting up. Her hand brushed across my stomach, and then I saw her standing, a dark shape against the moonlit window.

"Do you suppose your roommate could drive me home?"

"What?"

"Do you suppose Jeff could drive me home?"

"Susannah, what is it? I don't understand what happened. What did you want to say? Why can't you sleep with me?"

"Xavy, I like you. I said I did."

"Why won't you stay?"

"I've thought something out," she said, "and it's a decision I've made."

"But what's wrong?"

"We'll have a chance to talk about it."

"But now," I said.

She was putting on her dress.

"Susannah?" I stood up and put my arms around her. Her dress felt strange against my skin. She stepped back.

"Would Jeff mind?" she said.

"I don't think he would, he's such an agreeable bloke."

At that point I had no sense of what had happened. I simply knew I wanted her in my bed all night. I decided she was probably a lot less serene than I had taken her for and she felt guilty about sex when it happened so easily, when she knew me so slightly.

"I'll just knock on his door," she said.

"Oh, I'll ask him," I said. "I'll get his keys. I'll take you back."

She was firm. "No, Xavy," she said. "I don't want you to."

I plunked down on the bed, she kissed my forehead, said good-night, and went out. I had been feeling quite elated, but now I started to fall.

When I heard her tap on Jeff's door, I suddenly had one of my visions of the old supercool Jeff sweeping her into his arms. I am sure in reality he just stumbled into a pair of jeans, blinkily opened the door, and very politely, without asking any questions, took her home.

But I did not hear anything. The fact is, my head was buried in my pillow. It had hit me all of a sudden when I heard her tap on his door, the old paranoia, the whole horrible thing.

I have been left other times, before and since. This time was the worst, and even now I am not sure why it was. I cannot recall exactly what hopes I had put in Susannah in the earlier part of the evening, but, whatever they were, her leaving did away with them. I must have been hoping for a small break, an upturning — I was ready to raise my stunted expectations if someone would put up with me for a little while. But that is a poor excuse. If I had truly wanted to, I would have made my own break, my own upturning. I do not think I had seriously considered that I might actually *keep* Susannah. I had taken her to bed without thinking of that.

When Jeff came back I was sitting in his wicker chair in his room in a numbed state with a bright red towel wrapped around me.

"Do you have any idea what she was upset over?" I said, sounding very calm.

He sat on the edge of the desk and looked at me. His

expression was strict and serious. With a tilt of his head he said, "You've got to be more careful, Xavy."

"What did she tell you?"

"Nothing. She didn't want to talk. But I know you, Xavier Fereira."

"You're a great help, Jeff," I said. I was too numb to argue with him. He would only make me feel more deserted and pointless, and there was no reason to defend myself.

Jeff did not realize till the morning that I had fallen into one of my worst depressions. I went into my room and looked at the white sheets crinkled on the bed in the moonlight. For some odd reason, perhaps as a punishment, I decided to sleep on the floor.

2

I took the whole weekend off and finally managed to get somewhere with a mindless girl named Yvonne Morris whom I have been casually involved with recently. But I told her she had to leave at ten this morning because I had work to do. There was once a time when I never asked anyone to leave, but now that I am writing this book I find it is quite easy to be alone. I am experiencing the first fruits of therapy, says Lichty.

When I dropped out of college in 1965, I went to see a doctor named Pitts, but he was an unsympathetic man, and I should have suspected nothing would come of seeing him. He merely wanted to help me moderate my notions and make me more acceptable in the order of things. Dr. Lichty is a man of greater spirit. He

31

knows my ambition is not merely to be acceptable, but to be admirable. Anyone can be accepted if he compromises himself enough, but he will be admired only if he expresses himself. I do not think Dr. Pitts saw anything in me particularly worth expressing. It was a matter of calming me down and fitting me in.

Susannah could not have known when she left my room that I was at all shaky psychologically. I had practically forgotten it myself, things had been going so well, and it surprised me, too.

It was the worst depression Jeff had seen me in. I had been rather well-balanced since we first roomed together, so it frightened him considerably. I was scared by his physical attacks, he by my psychological ones. It is odd I should have felt that he had the better body and I the better mind.

I decided to take myself to a clinic and look into the possibility of getting back into therapy. Jeff came along for support. I had no intention of returning to Pitts, but I knew I needed to see someone. I remember sitting in a dark Victorian hallway with a huge mahogany-framed mirror on the wall facing us. I was small, dark, and looked worried. Jeff was long, fair, and stern. I stared into my own eyes in the mirror while he read a dog-eared copy of *Walden*.

I was seen by a Dr. Regenschirm who calmed me down and suggested I join a therapy group, but I insisted on seeing him again privately. I saw him three times and finally decided I could handle things on my own. For two years my skeptical parents, with much urging from my senior tutor, had sent me money for Pitts, and I had nothing to show them for it. It is true he had been someone to talk to when I had no one else, but the essential situation had obviously remained. It unearthed itself when Susannah left my room that night.

So I continued in a mildly draggy state for three months. I lost my job (lost it, not quit it, as I said in Chapter One — I must be entirely truthful), but I still read, listened to music, and had a little passing sex when I could get it. I cut off all my friends but Jeff and Susannah, and even they did not see much of me.

Perhaps I should get off myself for a while. I have set out to tell the story of my friendship with the two of them, but I know little of their private times together, and that limits me. I am certain they did not fall into bed immediately, though they must have been sleeping together by November. I sometimes wondered if Jeff was undersexed, but that was foolish. He simply gave himself enough else to do to keep him from depending on one easy source of gratification. Jeff was as sexually minded as I was, but sex did not control him. Still his self-control sometimes struck me as a little inhuman.

In any case, Jeff did not need to track down Susannah right away. But he did call her up to ask her advice about his depressed roommate, and that is how they began to fall in love. It must have been odd, falling in love discussing a third person, but perhaps they saw each other in a better perspective that way.

At first Jeff did not say much to me about it for fear of setting me off. I am sure that many times when he said he was working on his research project, he was actually on Beacon Hill with Susannah. He was away from the apartment a good deal. Perhaps he simply could not stand seeing me hang around the place. I had some rather paranoid fantasies that he was just waiting for an opportunity to tell me he was moving out. Still, he did spend hours talking to me, thinking of things for me to do — he gave me money, he invited me out to Chicago. But then he stayed away for days at a time saying he was doing research in Roxbury and was sleeping in some project office. Perhaps it was true.

Susannah and I did not talk about what had happened between us until February, but the three of us did spend some pleasant evenings together, listening to records at our apartment or over at the Music Building where there was a piano. Jeff's expectations sank when he first heard Susannah play. He had been expecting a second Myra Hess, I suppose, but at the same time he must have been somewhat relieved that his future wife, as he was already imagining her, was not going to be a concert star.

Susannah's touch was sure enough, and she had learned quite a difficult repertory, but she did not have the architectural sense of how to control a piece of music. The first movement of the Schubert rambled about.

34

The themes came through with feeling, but the other notes were treated merely as what came in between — she never took hold of them. The Ravel was very bad. She did not have the technique for it, nor did she have power enough for the great chords in the Brahms. Her Beethoven, the twenty-seventh sonata, was the best. The pretty tune in the second movement suited her.

But all her grace and serenity disappeared when she reached a difficult passage. She became very earnest and sat awkwardly hunched over the keys, breathing in nervous little gasps. Jeff suggested she save the Schumann for another time because he did not want to tire her. I doubt that Susannah sensed his disappointment in her playing, which after all had been perfectly adequate by amateur standards. She probably did not realize that Jeff had been counting on more artistry.

One Saturday in late October, the three of us decided to drive up to Mount Monadnock. Jeff's pale blue Sprite, the model with the froggy headlights, only seated two, so Susannah had to sit on my lap. She was excited, not having climbed a mountain since she was a teenager in West Virginia, and had dressed for a real hike: sneakers, jeans, and her brother's green Marshall University sweatshirt. The color suited her because of her eyes.

Though she was on my lap, the alliance had shifted, and I was conscious of holding another fellow's girl. Not that she belonged entirely to Jeff yet, but she was clearly not mine anymore. She was very taken with the little towns, the rocky pastures, and turning leaves. It was my home territory, or rather the aristocratic countryside which surrounds my home territory, and I felt no place could be as beautiful. We made a jolly trio and fooled around, tweaking and tickling, as if we were back in high school. It was the kind of regression you resort to now and then as you grow into your twenties.

The mountain was not crowded. Jeff and I had climbed it in the summer with Elly and a girl I had been chasing after named Alison. Then it had been swarming with day campers and outdoorsy families, but now we saw only a few other hikers. The weather was no longer warm.

Monadnock is a lone mountain which rises out of the rolling countryside of southern New Hampshire. The various trails to the top follow rocks where water rushes down in the spring. The trails are steep enough to provide some good exercise but are by no means difficult.

Jeff generally took the lead, and I brought up the rear. At one point I asked him if he had thought to bring his adrenalin inhaler, and he said he had not. I said he must have a death wish. It was when he exercised and got hot in cold weather that he often had attacks. I could see Jeff flinging himself about on the rocks on top of the mountain. There would not have been much we could do for him up there.

"I haven't had an attack in a year," he said, "not since that soccer game."

Susannah was concerned, so I went into the details

of Jeff's allergies. He played them down as always, and I dramatized them considerably. Susannah got the idea there was quite a serious problem. "They say asthma is basically emotional," she said.

"It's not really asthma," said Jeff. "It's called urticaria."

"Which is even worse, dope," I said. "And it really is partly emotional, Kimberk, I'm sure it is, whatever you say."

"Maybe it is. I'm not going to get into an argument about it." Jeff always avoided discussing his irrational elements.

Susannah quickened her pace to keep up with him. I remember him saying several times, "Come on, Fereira, you slowpoke," which only made me fall farther behind. I soon had to look for the white dots painted on the rocks to mark the trail because Jeff and Susannah were out of sight. I would see them climbing over a boulder or coming out of a patch of trees, but they soon disappeared again. At one point I saw them holding hands, and my remaining spirit left me. I wanted to sit down and quit, but I did keep on. When I think of myself at that stage of my life I am terribly embarrassed. The pouty whininess, the draggy dispiritedness — it was rather revolting. I allowed other people's self-sufficiency to defeat me so easily.

The top of Monadnock is bare rock. Jeff and Susannah waited for me before the final stretch, and we all reached the top together. The little hut up there was maintained through October, so we were able to get some hot chocolate and cookies. Then we sat on the highest boulder and looked across the orange and brown landscape. It was cold and windy, and we all huddled together with Susannah in the middle.

She was very excited but did not gush as I recall Alison doing when she first saw the quite different green landscape in the summer. Susannah conveyed her enthusiasm with her eyes and by crinkling up her cheeks in a smile. Then she got up and leaped about the boulders as if in time to some grand orchestral finale. Jeff followed her, and I sat and watched them from the highest rock, which had the elevation carved into it.

The way down was steeper. We took the white arrow trail which followed dusty gullies and dry waterfalls. At times we sat down and simply slid. At the bottom I offered to do the driving back to Boston which gave Jeff a chance to have Susannah on his lap. It was only fair. I would have felt funny with her at that point anyway, for I had become quite gloomy on the way down the mountain.

We had a big fight about stopping for food. I kept overshooting all the Dairy-Freez stands, but finally we saw one in time to slow down, and we stuffed ourselves with Jeff's favorite kinds of cellophane-wrapped goodies.

Driving into town after dark, we fell silent. I remember the yellow full moon in the upper left-hand corner of the windshield. It made me all the sadder and quieter, and I thought of how the friend I had finally caught up to after years of trailing after had speeded up again and left me all the more convinced of my slowpokery. Such melancholy swept over me often in those months. It was no surprise when Mr. Thatcher let me off the job. He was pleasant enough about it. I had not been enlivening the place very much, and I suppose he thought customers sensed my mood and did not buy as many paperbacks.

I could not pay the December rent. Jeff gave it to me as an advance Christmas present and included an additional forty dollars to make an even hundred. I told him I would pay him back as soon as possible, but he said he did not want a debt hanging over our friendship and gave me the money outright. He thought he was helping matters, but, as Dr. Lichty has since pointed out, the gift has hung over us more destructively than any debt might have. I felt very guilty about taking the money, but I did not have the willpower to go out and get another job right away. It may even have been more sinister than that. Perhaps I had managed to make Jeff feel guilty for having a trust fund and he was assuaging his conscience with the gift.

I scarcely remember what I did with my time. I must have listened to a lot of records and read a lot of books, and I think I was more sex-obsessed than usual, but I do not remember Carol or Darlene or any of the other girls I was trailing after except by their names in my diary. I kept a diary at the time because it seemed to provide everything a psychiatrist could. Dr. Pitts had left me with the impression that psychiatrists simply sat in their leather chairs and looked at you while you told them who you wanted to lay.

Jeff's boss gave him a full Christmas vacation, and Susannah went home to see her parents. I planned to be at home myself, as I had been every past Christmas of my life. My sister Susie was engaged to Robin Mc-Phee, a boy from her high school class. In January he was shipping off to Nam (his word for it), and my parents were anxious to have us all together rallying around Susie and Robin. But then Jeff suggested I drive out to Illinois with him and see another part of the country for once. I made the selfish choice because I did not feel like facing my big unreasonable family in my depressed state.

My mother was especially hurt by my decision, and my father took it angrily. Neither of them could understand what I was doing with my life anyway (Jeff said I could hardly blame them). Susie was disappointed and cried over the phone. Things had been strained between us since Jeff ran over Aztec, and she felt I no longer cared about her. Lucy and Tony were disappointed too. I suppose only Mike and his wife Linda were just as glad I would not be around adding to the confusion.

The day before Jeff and I left, I borrowed his car and drove up to my parents' house with a box of stupid presents: a book on Latin American revolutionary movements for my father and a fancy Parisian cookbook for my mother (both presents were subtly designed to provoke the recipients), a letter-writing kit for Susie (she would need it with Robin going away, but it was an unhappy kind of present — I should have given her perfume), an orange birdcage cover for Mike and Linda, a record by the Screaming Goons for Tony, and a stuffed hippopotamus for Lucy. My mother told me she was having my present shipped. It was waiting in the hallway when we got back from Chicago: a big gray package containing an electric waffle iron. My mother always sent me expensive things I did not need.

It was a long uninteresting drive west. The turnpike and rest areas were the same for a thousand miles. I had not expected so much new countryside to be so boring. We took turns at the wheel and made it in eighteen hours. Somewhere around Fort Wayne, late at night, I began to feel mildly agoraphobic seeing how flat it was, and I was also quite nervous about meeting Jeff's parents.

We reached the Kimberks' house after midnight. The weather was cold, but there had been no snow yet. I had only a vague impression of the house in the darkness with tall pines and hedges around it and a semicircular gravel driveway. It was a Victorian house with a wide verandah and a cupola. I had no preconception of Jeff's parents themselves, but somehow I had been expecting them to live in one of those pseudo-Tudor houses with gateposts that you see in rich suburbs.

Jeff had seldom talked about his parents, and the one time I had expected to meet them, at our graduation, they had been off in Peru. Jeff had not seen them since spring vacation when he had joined them on Sanibel Island in Florida for ten days.

There was a dim light in the front bay window. Mr. Kimberk came out on the verandah and greeted us as we climbed up the steps. He shook Jeff's hand, something my father never did with me, and then shook mine and seemed very glad indeed to meet me. I soon lost the shakiness that had been building up inside me on the pike as we neared Chicago.

We left our suitcases beneath the stairs in the entrance hall and went into the front parlor where there was a dying fire in the fireplace and an unlighted Christmas tree standing in a corner. I could not immediately identify the piece of music that was playing, but it was very familiar.

Jeff and I sat down in the soft blue armchairs by the fire, and Mr. Kimberk suggested a glass of port. Then he pulled up a wooden rocker, which he said was good for his back, and we began to talk. He was a soft-spoken man, about fifty, long-legged, red-faced, with a moustache, a pipe, and smudges of purple veins on his cheeks. I could see the family resemblance.

Mr. Kimberk was curious about Jeff's job, and I was glad to hear more about it myself. I am ashamed to say that in my depressed state I had taken little interest in Jeff's goings on. It turned out he was coordinating his sociological research with a neighborhood self-help project in Roxbury. He taught classes and at the same time made a psychological study of the people he was teaching.

I sat silently and sipped my port, but when Mr. Kimberk turned to me and asked what I had been doing lately, I panicked slightly. I explained I was not as socially motivated as Jeff seemed to be and had just been working in a bookstore. Mr. Kimberk puffed at his pipe, and we let the subject pass. I imagined he knew about the hundred dollars Jeff had given me and thought ill of it, and though I could detect no resentment from him, my paranoia told me it must be there.

Jeff asked about his mother and his sister Zada (they had already gone to bed) and about various relatives and friends. Then his father brought out an album of pictures of the trip to Peru, and we spent a long time familiarizing ourselves with Machu Picchu and Ollantaytambo and such places. Jeff held the album on his lap, and I went over and sat on the arm of his chair. His father stood behind us pointing out things with his pipestem. I liked Mr. Kimberk and regretted I did not have anything especially lively to add to the conversation. My depression had got me out of the habit of taking an active interest in things.

The Kimberks were great travelers with a particular interest in pre-Columbian culture. They had gone to Yucatan several times to pick around in the jungle, and though Mr. Kimberk contended it was nothing more than a hobby, he had many friends in the archaeology department at the University of Chicago, and it seemed he really knew his subject. In the course of my visit I learned the names of all the important sites but have since forgotten them. I do remember Mr. Kimberk said that the Palace of the Governors at Uxmal was, in his opinion, the handsomest building in the western hemisphere. He pulled out his Yucatan album to show me, and I had to agree.

As we talked on, it puzzled me more and more that Jeff had told me so little about his parents. I looked at Mr. Kimberk closely as he sat in his rocker and tapped his pipe on the edge of a pewter ashtray. When I asked him how he had the time to do so much traveling and still be a lawyer, he just smiled. It has puzzled me ever since.

We finished our port, and the record (I felt stupid for not having identified it sooner as the "Archduke" trio) came to an end. As we got up to go to bed, we heard a soft, high-pitched voice at the top of the stairs. It was Mrs. Kimberk in a somewhat ratty pink bathrobe. She was plump and friendly looking. Jeff picked up his suitcase and went up ahead of his father and me and kissed his mother on the cheek.

"I'm sorry I came out looking like a slob," she said, "but I heard your voices, and I couldn't resist peeking out. It's been so long, Jeff." She gave him another hug, let him go, and then stretched out her hand to me, apparently as glad to meet me as her husband had been, but I was still telling myself they both must resent me underneath.

We talked a while on the narrow balcony, and then Mrs. Kimberk declared we must be exhausted after the drive. "Come along, you two, and I'll show you your quarters. And take your time tomorrow morning. Breakfast at any hour you please."

We all said good-night. I slept in the guest room in a big soft bed, and it was really too soft. I was used to sleeping on the hard lumpy mattress that had come with my brass bed, and though I was very tired I could not fall asleep for some time. I turned on the light again and looked through the books that were in the room. There was a shelf of old cartoon books (Helen Hokinson, Charles Addams, and Whitney Darrow, jr.) which I looked through for what may have been several hours. I am generally ill at ease in strange surroundings and feel the urge to snoop around, opening every cupboard and drawer, though I have never found anything out of the ordinary.

It was eleven o'clock when I came down for breakfast. Jeff had just got up himself. Mrs. Kimberk was standing at the stove in the warm kitchen, wearing khaki pants and a cashmere sweater (at least I will call it cashmere: she was an odd dresser and always matched something elegant with something plain).

During breakfast Zada came in from her riding lesson, and she was a bit of a disappointment to me at first. I had anticipated a pretty girl, and since Jeff only had shown me the picture of her as a little girl that he carried in his wallet, I suspected he was purposefully keeping her under wraps now that she was a seventeen-year-old knockout. But although she had a sweet face and beautiful round brown eyes, Zada was a bit horsy, not particularly tall, but ill-proportioned and still awkward. She wore riding boots and carried a little black velvet hat. Her jodhpurs (I learned the term from her later) made her bottom fan out like a pancake, and her long brown hair was tied, fittingly enough, in a pony tail.

Jeff was offhand with Zada, as I was with my sister Susie. They did not greet each other with a kiss or even anything more than a nod and a smirk. Jeff introduced us and asked Zada if she had seen his Sprite.

"Yeah, it's real neat," she said. Her voice had a nervous chortle in it.

Jeff suggested he take her for a quick ride.

"Go ahead, I'll keep Xavy company," said Mrs. Kimberk pulling up a chair across the breakfast table from me and pouring herself some coffee.

The table was on a sunporch overlooking the driveway. We watched brother and sister outside admire the car and then drive off. In the daylight I discovered that the Kimberks' lawn was clumpy and patchy and that the surrounding darkness, which had seemed so imposing the night before, had been supplied by shaggy overgrown hedges and straggly pines. Mr. Kimberk obviously did not employ a gardener. And the house was not elaborate inside either, nor did it show any signs that its inhabitants were fanciers of architecture. It was only a big, airy house, somewhat untidy, but comfortable. All this was a surprise to me.

Mrs. Kimberk stirred cream and sugar into her coffee and said she would have to fatten Jeff and me up while we were there. Though she had delicate features, she was simply too round to be considered pretty, and her body wobbled slightly when she moved. She asked me about my family, and I enumerated my brothers and sisters. "Big Catholic family," I said.

We got onto other things: the depressed economic state of New England's mill towns; city politics in general; Chicago; the buildings of Mies van der Rohe and Louis Sullivan which I must see; the Art Institute; the Symphony; what the program was that week; the maiden aunts who shared the box at Orchestra Hall with the Kimberks — they were nice, intelligent, comfortable people; and how Mrs. Kimberk hoped we would spend a lot of time around home so she could enjoy our company and we could take it easy. It came clear to me that Jeff had told his mother something of my nervous and depressed state and that she was hoping to be of help.

I heard about the countryside I must see, it being so different from New England. Jeff would drive me out to the Rock River valley and perhaps on to the Mississippi, Galena, the bluffs in Iowa. I might not find it as beautiful as she did, but for her the hibernating cornfields, the rolling meadows touched with snow, were aw-fully beautiful.

Then she got onto Jeff. She did not mean to pry, but she wondered how he was doing and how I thought he felt about things in general. I said I thought he was doing pretty well.

"I suppose you know he's no letter writer," she said, "and I have a hard time telling if he's all right. He'd never tell us if he wasn't."

"That's Jeff for you," I said. "He doesn't like to talk about himself."

"Well, he's so mysterious," said Mrs. Kimberk. It soon came out that what was puzzling her the most were the scattered references Jeff had made to a girl named Susannah Twombley. She was very curious but embarrassed for asking.

I said Susannah was a girl from West Virginia who taught piano in Roxbury and with whom Jeff was involved to some extent, but I did not know how serious he was. "Jeff never tells me anything either," I said.

"He's such a puzzle to us, Xavy. We only see him every six months or so, and he changes so in between." She spread orange marmalade thickly on a piece of rye toast and said she ate too much.

"I'm afraid I'm sort of responsible for his long hair," I said.

"Oh, I like it, I'm not at all against being shaggy. I think you've loosened him up a bit. He really used to

48

be too dapper for my taste. How about another pancake?"

Mrs. Kimberk was more keyed up than her husband. She talked nervously and was afraid of silences, but I was comfortable with her because she kept the conversation running easily along. With Mr. Kimberk I felt everything had its set pace, but Mrs. Kimberk's impulses directed her in a way that kept the talk fresh, and I felt whatever I might have to say would fit in.

I could not envision her in the jungles of Yucatan the way I could Mr. Kimberk, pith helmet and all, but Jeff told me later that his mother was very serious about their trips and was a great sport in the field. She always fell a bit behind and had to catch her breath frequently, but she had read a good deal and knew pre-Columbian history better than his father did, he said.

The Sprite returned. "That was quick," said Mrs. Kimberk as Jeff and Zada came up the back steps.

"I just remembered I said I'd call Cathy at twelve," said Zada. She clunked past in her riding boots and went upstairs. Jeff sat down at the table with us and poured himself some coffee. His mother made him some more pancakes too.

"How does Zada strike you, Jeff?" she said standing at the stove with her back to us. "She's very nervous about college."

"She'll get in. She's a brain."

"But, Jeff, it's harder than it was when you went through it. You have no idea how edgy she is. She wants

Vassar because she can ride there, but she also wants Radcliffe to be near you. She gets all steamed up and cries. Then she thinks it all doesn't matter because she won't get into either. Do you think you could calm her down?"

"Sure."

"And she's been so nervous about Xavy coming. She doesn't yet feel quite at ease with older boys."

"She has nothing to fear from me," I said, meaning to say I could not imagine myself frightening anyone, but as soon as I said it I realized it could be interpreted as a rude remark, and I felt uncomfortable.

Mrs. Kimberk wanted to hear about Jeff's research project, so we spent another half hour talking at the breakfast table. Then Zada came down and made herself lunch, and we sat around some more.

I grew to like Zada very much, and, once I got over my initial disappointment, I enjoyed looking at her and talking to her. Sex dominated my approach to girls at that time, so I should have been glad Zada was not a beauty. I might have carried on in my compulsive way and made a bad impression on the Kimberks and had a horrible time.

Zada was shy and schoolgirlish, but she really was as smart as Jeff had said and always won the Scrabble and Perquackey games we played in the evenings. It must have been difficult for her to have such a good-looking older brother. No one could avoid comparing them. I decided to buy her a bright and cheerful scarf or some such thing for Christmas.

Jeff and I went shopping in the city during the last-minute rush. After carefully investigating the Kimberks' library I bought a record for Mr. Kimberk (Clara Petraglia singing Brazilian songs) and a book for Mrs. Kimberk (*Victories in Defeats*). It was difficult to find a book or record they did not already own.

Jeff presented an even greater problem. I did not want to be extravagant since it was the money he had given me I was spending, but I did not want to appear cheap either. I decided he would like something useful rather than symbolic, so I got him a small filing cabinet.

The Kimberks all had presents for me: an astronomical paperweight, a pair of fuzzy llama slippers from Peru, and a white turtleneck sweater that was really quite expensive. Jeff gave me a handsome edition of *Os Lusíadas* in Portuguese. Though I would probably never try to read it, it was something I was rather glad to own.

Zada went overboard with her present for me. Nehru shirts had just come into style. This was a real Indian one of plain white cotton. I was very touched and thought the psychedelic scarf I had given her was awfully cheap and silly by comparison. But she tied it around her neck right away, and it spruced her up considerably. She still has it. I have seen her wearing it around the Square.

That was the most pleasant Christmas morning I can

remember, not chaotic like my family's Christmases. We all sat in the front parlor around the tall spruce decorated with ornaments Jeff and Zada had made when they were little: horrible sequined Styrofoam things and, from a later period, toothpick angels on cotton clouds. We opened the presents slowly, taking time to undo the ribbons and fold up the paper. Mrs. Kimberk kept a list of presents from relatives so everyone would know who to write thank-you notes to for what. There were lots of extravagant presents: art books and travel books, old pieces of china and lusterware, a rather bear-like winter coat for Zada. Jeff got the complete *Grove's Dictionary of Music*.

Mrs. Kimberk was pleased with the book I gave her, though she had never heard of it. Mr. Kimberk took a special interest in the Clara Petraglia record and played it right away. He said Brazil would have to be the next place they visited, to travel up the Amazon to Manaus, to see old Bahia and Pernambuco. "What do you say, Jeff, shall we all go?" he said. "And we can take Xavy along because he knows a little of the language." I had a sudden vision of all of us in Brazil on a sunny seaside terrace sipping Mateus around a little table.

At the time I felt anything was possible with the Kimberks and was convinced they truly liked me. Of course I felt most at ease with Mrs. Kimberk, while Mr. Kimberk remained somewhat intimidating. Yet he responded to the record and got me to translate snatches of it, and we went on to discuss Portuguese culture in general and the beauty of Lisbon, which I have never seen, provincial Down East type that I am. In time I came to interpret Mr. Kimberk's aloofness as a gentle trait, not a forbidding one.

And I soon grew used to the scale of things at the Kimberks'. I ate too much, slept too much, drank a bit too much, and more than anything we talked a great deal, but not too much, I should say. I had missed such conversation a long time.

Several nights after Christmas, an overdose of wine at dinner got me talking about psychiatry. By then I was even more at ease with the family, and I joked away about Dr. Pitts and Dr. Regenschirm and made light of the subject, which made it easier to talk about. Even so, I was well aware that the Kimberks believed strongly in psychiatry, for Jeff had once said I might change my low opinion of the profession if I were to see a doctor like his mother's former analyst, a woman named Dr. Helene Olafsson.

"Xavy," said Mrs. Kimberk, "I think you've just seen the wrong doctors." This was in the darkened dining room over coffee. The candles were still burning and had begun to drip, the water glasses were half empty, and we each had a dessert plate with a white puddle on it crossed by a large dessert spoon. The dessert had been blueberries and lemon ice.

"I think Bess is right, Xavy," said Mr. Kimberk. "A lot depends on how you get along with a doctor as a person. It's true of any human relationship."

"But it's not so much the doctor," I said. "I think there are certain things about yourself you just can't change." I discussed the evils of behaviorism, brainwashing, all that sort of thing. I was arguing, but not very seriously, and I did not feel nearly as inflexible as I had always felt with Jeff discussing the same subject. I was somewhat surprised at myself for discussing it with the Kimberks at all.

"Xavy, I think you're off the track," said Mr. Kimberk.

"I'm off my track all right," I said.

He knit his brow and took a sip of coffee. "It's a question of bringing out buried feelings which are nonetheless part of you," he said, "and then the apparent feelings will begin to change on the strength of the new feelings which have been released. But they're all your own feelings."

"You seem to think, Xavy," said Jeff, "that psychiatrists have some mystical power to change you, like magicians."

Zada asked if she could be excused to do some homework. Perhaps I was embarrassing her with my talk. The rest of us talked on, and finally it was Mrs. Kimberk who convinced me that it could not hurt to go talk to her old analyst and see if I got some ideas about what to do next.

"You need some sort of advice now, Xavy, don't you think? Dr. Olafsson would be easy to talk to. She has a way of seeing her way to the heart of a matter. You'll

54

be going back to Boston in a couple of days anyway, and, after all, you need never see her again."

It was part of my feeling of being in a new part of the country for the first time that made me receptive to whatever came up. There was also a certain weariness in remaining negative. Perhaps I had sunk as low as my spirit was going to allow me to. And there was also the fact I was mildly drunk.

The next morning Mrs. Kimberk made an appointment for me, and I felt rather good about it, but nervous, and I could not imagine how I would explain to this Dr. Olafsson what was wrong with me.

Jeff and I drove downtown on Friday morning, December twenty-ninth. I was to see the doctor and meet Jeff for lunch at the Art Institute afterwards. Then we were going to Orchestra Hall for a concert.

Dr. Olafsson's office had a plate-glass view of the park across Michigan Avenue and in the distance of the lake. She was a large woman and quite old, and she had a strong accent which gave her words a certain distinctness. I gathered she was Danish. Her broad bosom and square shoulders sat solidly behind her desk. On them stood her head. I put it that way because it was as striking a head as I have ever seen. Straight gray hair hung at the sides; parted in the middle on top. The forehead was high and flat, the nose extremely long and bulbous, the lips narrow. She was an ugly woman.

Like all psychiatrists she looked directly at me, but without demands, with plenty of time, content to wait and observe. Jeff later built my meeting with her into a great mystical experience, but that was Jeff's romantic side. To me the hour with Dr. Olafsson was entirely straightforward. There was nothing mystical about it. We took to each other, and perhaps that was all Jeff meant, but he inflated it so. We simply took to each other. The things I said came through to her, and she let me know she understood me just by nodding, by smiling, by saying "I see" and "Yes."

If I can remember it, she sat with the horizon of the lake behind her and the morning sun on the snow. It had snowed since Christmas. But in fact I think her desk was against a plain white wall. I have the strong memory of being on top of a high building with a frozen landscape on the other side of plate glass. Now I remember exactly how it was. I sat on a couch which faced the window. She sat at her desk which was to my right against a plain white wall. But she turned in her pivoted leather chair and watched me. My eyes went from her to the view of the lake and back again nervously. I superimposed both views in my mind and remembered her against the horizon, but she was against the wall.

I told her about Susannah, about Jeff, about my sister Susie and her fiancé, about my parents. I gave the chronology of my life, how I went off to prep school, to college, how I took a year off when things got bad, what I did that year, how Jeff and I became friends. I told her about my panic attacks and my depressions, all about Dr. Pitts, how I kept trying to "make girls"

56

as I put it (she understood the phrase), how many girls I had actually made, what future I saw for myself, what I wanted to do, that I might like to write a book or be a teacher or a social worker but none of them seemed right, that I still felt in awe of Jeff and Susannah and of their involvement with each other, that love seemed entirely out of my reach. Dr. Olafsson had little to say because I could not stop talking.

But she gave me some specific instructions. She told me to go back to Boston and see a man named Dr. Kevin Lichty whose address she gave me on a little orange slip. She said she would write him and give him her impressions of me and her recommendations for a course of treatment. He was with a state clinic, and the price could be adjusted to my budget. I need not ask my parents to pay.

"You are too fine," she said. "You must do this and see it through. You are warm and honest. I like you immensely." She made much of that last word. "Mr. Fereira, you have waited, and it was necessary, but the time has come. You need a push." She tightened her fist and grinned at me. "You are a gentle, sweet person, a loving person. I can see it. Perhaps you cannot. Lichty is a young man. I know him. I think you have had bad luck, but you will not with him. I think you really want to be a happy person and be yourself, not be constrained."

When the hour was up I shook her hand across the desk and thanked her for taking time to see me. She re-

mained seated. Her good-bye was very feminine. It was
as if her solidity had done its job. I suddenly thought
that here was a nice old woman in a skyscraper in Chicago who knew everything about me, and I would never
see her again.

Jeff and I had lunch in the Art Institute cafeteria.
I told him Dr. Olafsson had been very helpful, and he
was pleased. Later we celebrated by getting figuratively
drunk on Nielsen's Fifth. This being the second concert
of my visit I was on very jolly terms with Miss Wilsey
and Miss Whalen, Jeff's aunts who shared the box
with us.

Then Jeff and I drove back along the dark frozen
lake. I was glad to be with him on his home ground.
Things seemed solid between us again. We knew each
other and appreciated each other. My life had even
taken a turning: I had something specific to do when I
got back to Boston. It was then he felt he could tell me
he was in love with Susannah. Of course I had known it
for some time.

3

IT is the first of December, 1969. I have known Jeff more than seven years, which is a good portion of my life. But we only spent two years in close company, and I feel we will not see much of each other ever again. I will have to do without his companionship, and there will not be a chance to form such another friendship again. It becomes clear as I write this book that I am past the careless stage of life when I can spend most of my time doing things with my friends.

I seem to be taking only a week to write each of these chapters. It is going faster than I thought because I have kept at it and saved my relaxing for the weekends. This weekend I called up Yvonne Morris, but she was out, so I called up Zada. She is still much the same as she appeared in Chapter Two. I feel sorry for her and perhaps add to her frustration by being friendly, but I am fond of her and cannot help checking on her now and then. We went to a rerun of Olivier's *Othello*, but, as good as it was, I should have taken her to something silly. Zada always feels she must be intellectual with me because Jeff used to tell her how smart I was.

Jeff was always impressed by the way I had of writing a term paper from the top of my head a week after it was due, with all sorts of striking insights in it, while he took weeks trying to make sense of his ideas, which were always unorganized and contradictory. He had an academic conscience and would put everything down on three-by-five index cards and spread them out on the floor, arranging them one way, then another. Then he would draft the paper once and get so disturbed he would tear it up and do it again. It was a tedious process of rehashing until he finally had something which to him seemed coherent (but which usually still puzzled his teachers), and his endless B minuses made him feel like a meathead. My half-finished, unmotivated papers always outstripped his careful ones, and, undependable as I was, I had an aura of inspiration about me which angered Jeff, while it impressed him, and which excited Zada and made her afraid of appearing stupid when she was with me.

After the movie we had coffee and a sausage at the Zum-Zum and discussed the movie as serious young intellectuals do. All the time I knew that the most important thing for her was that she was out in the Square

with a fuzzy-headed older fellow, and the most important thing for me was that I was looking after my best
friend's sister.

I find money quite the problem I always have. When
I returned from Chicago two years ago, I had the January rent to pay, and my parents, who were entirely baf-
fled by my continuing aimlessness, grudgingly agreed
to start sending me a small allowance. Lichty and I have
been working at the financial question for some time
now, and we do not seem to have solved it in a permanent way. I have had some funny little jobs these past
two years, but it has gone no further than that.

When I took Zada out, she paid for herself. I wish I
could report to Lichty that I insisted on paying for
her, but I cannot. I make such sensible resolutions in his
office and then come out and act otherwise. I must be
needling him in an underhanded way, to prove I still
need his help.

I will have to return to the story now, much as I enjoy rambling on about myself. This is an important
chapter. It contains an event quite outside the ordinary
daily routine: two people will decide to commit themselves to each other's company for life.

Because their affair was finally out in the open, Jeff
and Susannah began to spend more time at the apartment. For a while they were hesitant even holding hands
in front of me, and the fact that I had just been dumped
by a girl named Darlene made me all the more depressed
the first time Susannah spent the whole night.

But by the end of January, we were all on comfortable terms again. In fact, a kind of taboo had grown up around Susannah, and I stopped thinking of her as a sexual object. On evenings when she was not at the apartment, Jeff would have long talks with me about her. It was always on the pretense of making sure I was not upset by his involvement, but all he really wanted was to talk about Susannah with someone. His fresh enthusiasm, previously one of his attractive qualities, now began to upset me. It stood in such healthy contrast to the thoughtlessness of what I had done back in September.

"Hey, Xavy," said Jeff one cold January afternoon. "Come in here, would you?"

I got off my bed, where I was lying reading *The Torrents of Spring* (still on a Turgenev kick), and went into Jeff's room, which he kept a lot colder than mine. The filing cabinet I had given him sat open on the floor, and Jeff was on his mattress with one hundred pink questionnaires for his project distributed about him in various piles. I sat down too heavily in the wicker chair, and it creaked.

"Watch the chair!" he said.

"It's what you get for buying junky furniture."

"It's what I get for having a clod for a roommate."

"What's eating you?" I said.

"All these fucking questionnaires." Jeff used that particular participle a good deal.

"Well, what can I do about them?"

"It's all the tabulating."

"Why can't you just ask me please to help you, if that's what you're getting at?"

"It really wouldn't take very long," said Jeff, "if I read off results to you and you put them in the proper columns."

"Why can't you do that?"

"It'd take twice as long."

"You're getting paid for it," I said.

"Oh come on now, Xavy, what do you expect me to do, pay you for helping me?"

"I've got things of my own to do, Kimberk."

"What? Read a book? You don't have to do that."

He was perfectly right, but I said, "Reading is as crucial to me as any asshole research project is to you. Just because I don't get paid for it."

"You might think once about doing something you got paid for."

"Hey, I don't have to sit here and listen to this shit," I said. I got up and left and slammed the door and lay around my room in a mood. At times Jeff had me totally convinced he was a better man than I was.

But in a short while, he opened my door and stuck his head in. I looked over at him. His red-faced anger had been replaced by sheepishness.

"Now what?" I said in an irritated voice.

"Sorry, Xavy. I was being a turd. You see, I was trying to get everything done so I could have the evening free with Susannah."

"Selfish old Jeff," I said. I was able to sneak out with criticisms of him only when he was being repentant.

He sat down on the end of the bed and leaned uncomfortably against the brass bedstead. Now he had an empty look on his face. "I know I'm selfish," he said, "but I've got to be able to spend some time with her tonight."

I gave in and helped him tabulate his results. Of course I owed it to him, not just for the money he had given me and the furniture he had bought for the apartment and the times he let me use his car, but also for the good feelings between us. And I really had nothing better to do.

Jeff and Susannah are living in Chicago now, and they are not having an easy time at all. Something cruel in me does not feel as sorry for them as it should. I suppose it is my way of making up for having been unduly impressed by them at one time. Not that I am free of their influence now. Indeed, as long as I devote my energies to writing this book I will be paying them both a strange kind of tribute.

I do not mean to sound entirely negative. When I think back to living with Jeff, I have pleasant memories for the most part. Now I live alone and find it tremendously difficult, but I am too old to put up with a communal gang of unreliable roommates, and too particular. Even I, who used to revolt at Jeff's nest building, actually get disturbed by people who come over and hang around, leaving dirty dishes and records on the floor. I am not capable of cooperative living anymore.

But I am not ready for anything else either, as my half-hearted involvements with females prove. Take Yvonne Morris: she is a local girl, a recent graduate of Somerville High who works in an office running a Xerox machine. I met her at the laundromat down the street, and she seemed attractive enough. But how I ever deluded myself into thinking there was any good reason for us to get to know each other I do not know. At least I am only capable of deluding myself for short periods of time.

I mentioned earlier the very rational discussion Susannah and I finally had on the subject of *our* little sexual episode. Let me get to that now.

Jeff and I had just turned twenty-three. Susannah gave us a double birthday party with a cake she and Ida Lee Sims had baked in the shape of a groundhog. It took some guessing on our part to identify what it was, but once we were oriented, we could pick out the nose and ears and paws.

Ida Lee Sims was a tight little thing, utterly self-confident, who shouldered herself around with a splashy sort of ease. All I really noticed was her long white-blond hair and her huge breasts. She played the violin, and she and Susannah had worked up the "Rain" sonata of Brahms as a special birthday surprise after dinner. The performance was what you might call loosely put together. Ida Lee's violin kept going astray, but she was very nonchalant about it. Susannah, on the other hand, kept wincing. She was a much more serious musician than her roommate.

On the strength of that evening, I decided to drop in casually one afternoon a week later when Ida Lee might be there alone. I gathered from Jeff that he and Susannah would be down in the project office all day, so I took the M.T.A. to Charles Street and made my way up Beacon Hill.

I pushed their outside buzzer and was greatly relieved when the doorlatch clicked and I could step into the warm hallway. I seem to be abnormally sensitive to cold temperatures. That day I had on two sweaters, one being my Christmas turtleneck, and a denim jacket, but I had lost my only pair of gloves, and my fingers were numb.

When I got to the fifth floor, still shivering with cold but flushed from the heat of the hallway, I expected to find myself alone with Ida Lee Sims, certain aspects of whom I had not been able to dispel from my thoughts. But it was Susannah who opened the door.

"Susannah! Oh, are you both . . ."

"No, we're not, Xavy, come in. Jeff's in Roxbury."

I stepped into the room, and she walked over and knelt on the window seat and looked out at the pale sky and the rooftops.

"I was sitting here gloomily and saw you stumbling up the hill," she said. "Have a seat."

I was still standing up taking off my jacket and having a hard time unbuttoning the buttons with my numb

66

fingers, so Susannah came and helped me. When I looked at her, I could see she was indeed in a glum mood.

"Oh, I'm depressed, Xavy-doo," she said.

When I finally got out of the jacket, she put her arms around me and held on for a bit. She was wearing a big bunchy gray sweater and seemed on the verge of tears.

"What's this Xavy-doo?" I said.

"Xavy, I'm glad you're around. You put things in perspective."

"What do you mean, perspective? You keep saying things you don't explain."

"Poor unenlightened creature," she said, hugging me tighter.

I did put my arms around her and tried to hold her in a comforting way. Then she let go of me and went back to the window seat. I sat down on the piano bench. The girls' apartment was a warren of tiny rooms under the eaves of a five-story brick town house and was eccentrically arranged in rooms shaped like Ls and Ts.

"You're really low, Susannah," I said. "You're acting almost silly, you're so low."

"That's right," she said.

"Why aren't you with Jeff?"

"Oh, he had a lot of work. Nothing for me to do really. I thought I'd come home and practice. Are you terribly disappointed you found me instead of Ida Lee?"

"Who says I was coming to see Ida Lee?"

"I can see right through you, Xavy-doo," she said, drumming her fingers on the windowpane. I noticed she had been drawing circles in the frost around the edges.

"Hey, listen, Susannah, what's got into you? You look so tense."

"Jeff asked me to marry him."

My chest got hot and a shiver went down my arms to my fingertips. She should not have told me so casually. She really should have let Jeff tell me. I got a little choked up. "Jeff did?" I said. Or something like that. I cannot remember what I said. There is a blank space in the scene here. That moment still makes me feel funny.

We were suddenly serious. "Let me get you some tea to warm you up, and we'll talk about it," she said and disappeared around the corner of the L.

I rubbed my eyes and tried to keep tears from coming. I played a chord on the piano. I cannot play but like to try out different combinations of keys as if searching for the Lost Chord, as the song goes.

Soon Susannah came back with a tray. There was a fat red teapot on it and two blue mugs, also a plate with three powdered doughnuts.

"Two doughnuts for you, Xavier Fereira," she said. She was brighter-eyed now, sitting in the black rocker with a red and green plaid blanket around her legs. "I hate this cold weather," she said.

I sipped at the tea and relaxed somewhat. "When did Jeff ask you?" I said.

"Last night. I shouldn't have said anything to you yet, Xavy. Please don't tell him. At least not till I decide."

"Decide what?"

"What I'm going to tell him."

"You mean you didn't just say yes?"

"Why do you think I'm so gloomy today?"

"There's a lot I don't know, Susannah."

"I'm sorry I said anything, Xavy. I couldn't help it." She gave me a smile that put things back in place for a moment. It was her old collected smile, her serene smile. She looked very Appalachian in the rocker.

"What did you mean I keep things in perspective?" I said.

"Is that what I said?"

"Something about perspective."

"I suppose I meant you're good at calming me down."

"I got the feeling you meant something more than that," I said.

"I don't know."

"I don't know. You were talking about being depressed."

"Well, I am."

"I thought you meant something like I put your depression into perspective because I have such extreme ones of my own. I was just going to say . . ."

"No, I'm sure I didn't mean that." She laughed, and

69

her voice took a sharper tone. "I don't think your depressions are anything to rave about, Xavy."

"Well, I don't mean rave about . . ."

"You always act, Xavy, as if there was something special about your mental condition. I don't think you've got it worse than anyone else." Her lips tightened up, and she looked at me with a suddenly fiery expression.

"What's got into you, Susannah? You're so edgy."

"Sometimes you make me very mad, Xavy. You really do. You wander around moaning and groaning about being so unmotivated and unable to fall in love. I'm supposed to think you have special problems and your condition is worse than mine or Jeff's or Ida Lee's. I know perfectly well what you were thinking coming over here, figuring how to chalk up Ida Lee on the scoreboard. That's your own stupid fault. Maybe you're right about perspective. You do put things in perspective. Not my depression either. But you put Jeff in perspective. When I see him in relation to you."

I got up and went around the corner and looked for the bathroom. When I found it, I closed the door and sat down on the edge of the tub and put my head in my hands for a while.

But soon Susannah came to the bathroom door and tapped lightly on it.

I said, "What?"

"Can I come in?"

"Yes."

The door opened and she came in. She had pulled the blanket around her like a shawl. "Come back in the living room, Xavy. I'm sorry."

I got up and followed her. We resumed our seats, picked up our teacups, and began the rational discussion I mentioned at the end of Chapter One.

"I'm ashamed of myself," said Susannah.

"That's all right. I'm ashamed of myself too."

"But I shouldn't pick on you like that," she said. "I've got myself in hand now."

"But you were right," I said. "I did come over to try to make it with Ida Lee, or at least get a start on her. And I'm aware of my gross shortcomings, but I'm finally getting on to new things with this doctor I've got now, and I'm sorry if I'm still acting adolescently, really, Susannah. I'll get over it in time."

"I didn't mean it like that, Xavy. And I certainly don't care what you try with Ida Lee. I'll just warn you she's not such a pushover as I was."

"Oh, I never get anywhere anyway. Just sort of wondered what it'd be like between those bosoms." We were back in our friendly way of joking. I shrugged my shoulders and smiled. "Tell me one thing, Susannah. We've never talked about it. Why did you go home that night after we had sex?"

She looked at me rather blankly for a moment and then said, "I was just protecting myself. You know? I was quite susceptible to you. I thought you were very attractive. But sort of needy. Well, you know, Xavy, you *were* needy. Of course you're getting better, but you were. Don't get mad." She got up and gave me a friendly kiss on my cheek.

"What's this?"

"I'm just feeling affectionate."

"I thought you were feeling depressed."

"Oh, I am. I just don't know what I'm going to say to Jeff." She sat back in the rocker and pulled the blanket up around her. In the winter she was paler; her sunburn was gone. She seemed softer and frailer.

We each had two cups of tea, and I finished off the doughnuts. Later, I brought the conversation back to the night in September because I still did not really know what had made her leave.

"I was a little afraid of you," she said.

"What! Of me?" It had always seemed to me if a girl were to have been afraid of anyone it would have been Jeff. "But I'm harmless," I said.

"Poor Xavy-doo."

"I don't think I like this Xavy-doo."

"I do. It reminds me of Xanadu."

"Anyway, Susannah, I don't see why you were afraid of me."

She smiled but did not answer. "And me?" she said. "What made you act so detached with me?"

I honestly did not think I had acted detached. I had acted as I always did in a situation like that and as I assumed others acted.

72

"I guess I had already figured you'd end up with Jeff," I said.

"Good Lord, Xavy, you're a defeatist."

"I'm glad you're willing to grant me that."

"Xavy, I didn't mean to talk down your problems earlier. You know how worried Jeff and I have been about you. He's so happy you're seeing this new doctor. He really does care about you." She was rocking gently back and forth. It was the only motion in the room. "And so do I. You're our best friend."

"You're both my best friends too," I said.

Susannah smiled at me and kept rocking gently.

"What are you going to tell Jeff?" I said.

"I'm going to put it off for a while. For a month at least. Until spring."

"He'll be disappointed if you put it off."

"I don't think so," said Susannah. "Jeff has a funny faith in what's doomed to be. You know how he is."

I never did go back to Beacon Hill to try to catch Ida Lee alone. Susannah and Jeff kept to themselves for weeks, and Jeff never told me he had already proposed to her. At Easter, he went to Huntington to meet the Twombleys, but as far as I knew, things were still undecided.

I went home that week for a visit, my first in months. My parents were only glad to have me around until the novelty wore off, my older brother Mike gave me hell one evening for my unkemptness and laziness and for conning my father into sending me an allowance, and my sister Susie ignored me as much as she could. She had once been my best pal. But Lucy and Tony still thought I was an admirable older brother, and I was able to persuade my parents to let Tony come down to Somerville for the weekend, though they distrusted my influence on him. He was seventeen, Zada's age, and anxious to see what sort of life I led. I worried about Tony then and still do. He is awfully empty-headed, but perhaps it is just his age. Lucy is the only member of my family who shows signs of much intelligence.

I will not be able to end this chapter on a high note as I did the last two. The spring was simply not very interesting. Most of my energy went into the Lichty thing. By mutual agreement we had decided to postpone dealing with Romance and Profession, overwhelming subjects which I did not know how to get at. Instead, we concentrated on how I felt about my family, a subject that did not threaten my daily routine, but, as Lichty well knew, was at the base of my difficulties.

So with me thinking I had a temporary reprieve from the real stuff, and with Lichty knowing he was getting at it all the time, we got along quite well. I was amazed to discover how much I had to spout off against my parents — not just the standard complaints I had been making for years, but deeper, stranger things I had never been able to talk about before.

There is one more scene that belongs in this chapter. It is not a crucial one, but it might end the chapter pleasantly.

I had once suggested that Susannah come with me to see one of the fishing fleets up the coast. When the weather was turning warm again and we were all eager to get out, we put the Sprite's top down and I squeezed into the little space behind the seats. Jeff and Susannah had suggested I go with them for a Sunday drive.

I still had heard nothing about Susannah's decision and had not asked about it. I must have felt I was hardly ready for such a decision in my own life and should stay out of one in theirs. My only function was as a sort of comic relief (though I was not especially funny) while they ruminated seriously and privately over the possibility of marriage. A couple of weeks later, it was all decided.

It was a bright fresh day, but unfortunately, as we drove along enjoying the air, a state trooper spotted my curly head as it sailed by him perhaps two miles an hour faster than it should have. He took off after us, not because we were speeding but because we looked like persecutable long-haired types having a little too jolly a time.

Jeff clamped on a stern expression and steered over to the breakdown lane. Up strode the trooper and, with a porky snort, asked us who the hell we thought we were. I do not think Jeff had ever been confronted by the law before.

"What's your name, fella?" said the trooper.

"Jeffrey Kimberk."

"All right, Mr. Kimberg, step out of the car a minute."

"What's the problem?"

"Don't ask me what the problem is. You're the problem. That's what's the problem." He had the same awful New England accent I had grown up with.

Jeff got out of the car, red in the face. I only hoped he knew enough not to react, but Jeff was idealistic and his instinct for his rights was sometimes irrepressible. He stood by the car with his hands in his pockets as the trooper wrote some things down. I sat up on the trunk lid. Susannah was shaking, she was so nervous.

Then the trooper looked into the car, spied something, and before any of us knew what he was doing, he reached onto the floorboards and picked up some little pebbles. "These are cannabis seeds, and I could take you all into the station if I wanted to."

I laughed and put my hands in my pockets.

"What are cannabis seeds?" said Jeff. He honestly had not heard the term before.

"Come off it, Mr. Kimberg!"

Jeff was growing redder. "I do not know what cannabis seeds are, and I demand to know what I'm being stopped for."

Susannah got out of the car on the other side and went to pick wildflowers in the ditch beside the road.

"Cannabis is pot, Jeff," I said.

"That is not pot! Those are pebbles! What would I be doing with pot on the floor of my car!" The veins on his neck stood out, he was so furious. "Anybody can see those are pebbles!"

"That is pot, fella," said the trooper, and the truth is he could say it was and take us back to the station, get some real seeds from their safe, and tell the judge he caught us with the stuff.

"What am I being stopped for?" said Jeff.

"Calm down, Kimberk," I said.

"Your friend seems to know well enough what cannabis is. What's your name, fella?"

Before I could answer, Jeff said, "Xavier Fereira."

"Your hair's a safety hazard, Mr. Fereira, blocks his vision." The trooper was enjoying being clever. "Where you from, Fereira?"

"Somerville," I said.

"Oh, I thought you might be related to Miguel Fereira up where I come from."

"I am. Miguel Fereira, the alderman. He's my dad."

Jeff was beginning to calm down. The trooper really did not find it odd asking if I were related to Miguel Fereira. We talked about our mutual hometown, and Susannah came back with a bunch of wildflowers. We were almost playing a good-natured game now that everyone knew no one was getting arrested. Jeff was smiling and shaking his head, enjoying a private joke.

"Now listen, Mr. Kimberg, I'm giving you a warning only because I see you're from Illinois." He pronounced the S. "But you better slow down if you don't want trouble."

He wrote out the warning, Jeff got back in the car, and we all said good-bye in a cheery tone. Then the trooper revved up his cruiser and tore out onto the road.

We continued up the coast, ate lobster rolls in Marblehead, and then went across to Wingaersheek Beach. We ran and jumped and let waves chase us, and if I had had someone along for me it would have been a perfect afternoon. As it was, it was good anyway. By that time I was perfectly adjusted to the idea of Jeff and Susannah as a married couple. It seemed the only natural thing.

At sunset we went on to Gloucester harbor, bought hamburgs at a drive-in, and took them down to the wharf to sit and look at the boats. Many had Portuguese names and flew the Portuguese flag against the darkening sky; the others were Italian. We heard some fishermen speaking Portuguese to each other as they walked by us, and I felt somewhat like a returned expatriate, though of course my family had not been at home among fishermen since my grandparents' early years.

We stayed and talked until the stars came out. Then we drove home, slowly, and rather cold with the top down.

4

I called Yvonne Morris this weekend, and she told me she did not want to see me again, at least not for a while. Of course, I could still keep after her, but I do not feel like making the effort. It must be possible to abstain from all this pointless behavior. I need a celibate interlude if I am ever to build up my reserves for someone more serious, a new Susannah perhaps.

As for the old Susannah, ever since her short visit to Boston last month I have been waiting for a letter to find out how she and Jeff are. Zada hears things secondhand through her mother, but I do not know how much of it is Mrs. Kimberk's speculation.

The last letter I had from Jeff was a whole month before Susannah's visit, and it dealt mainly with his socialist idealism, with only a hint of Susannah's state of mind. Here it is:

8 October 1969

Xavy,

Thanks for the Philip presents. He seems to like the rhinoceros best, grabs at it all the time. Sorry I haven't taken more time to write, but you can imagine how hectic it is around here. Did my mother send you the Polaroids of Philip? What do you think of him?

You should see how we're living now, a different scene entirely. You'd be surprised at us. We're cutting down to just what we cannot do without. Even books and records. I weeded out all the second-rate stuff and left it at my mother's. And minimum furniture, clothing, etc. Of course Susannah has her new piano, and we have an AR system now, but no TV, no gadgets. Saving our money for concerts and plays and taking our time walking through the parks with the baby. Having sold Spritely is best of all. Am not dreading the winter for once.

I'm glad we've simplified things like this in time for Philip to benefit from the start. No material clutter to screw up his values. And we're going to be very careful about not indoctrinating him, if we can help it, with false competitiveness. It's because of my work, I suppose. I see a hell of a lot worse here than I ever saw in Roxbury. We don't want much for ourselves.

I even have a new theory about sports. Remember what a jock I was back before you really knew me? You must have started me thinking this way. And you better not be an evil uncle who sends baseball mitts or football helmets for Philip's birthdays! It isn't just war toys anymore, it's the whole competitive shit. If people went hiking or rowing instead, and not racing, just going along, endurance tests, we'd all be happier.

*When I think what pressure I grew up under at school to beat
people out.*

*Speaking of pressure, how are things with old Dr. Wichtig?
Aren't you about ready to terminate? But I suppose it takes
longer than it ought to. I wish you could come out here and see
Philip, and see us with him. We're different people. Of course,
Susannah was a little depressed after the birth. I suppose
that's normal. She seems better now, just a little tired still.
It's odd how little prepared she was for having a baby. I think
I may treat her to a weekend trip to Boston by herself, just
to see Ida Lee for a little female support (she really doesn't
have any girls to talk to around here). So you may be seeing
her sooner than you think. Don't you think it might do her
good to get away for a few days? My mother could take care
of the baby. I am afraid being a mother is pretty overwhelming at first.*

Well, maybe I'll see you sometime soon too, old Xavy.

Jeff

*(We've sent Zada some pictures too. Show her yours and get
her to show you hers. Do you think she likes school any better
this year?)*

I think Jeff's idealism is getting a little farfetched.
Admittedly it would be hard even to get me into a game
of Frisbee, but anticapitalism is hardly the excuse I
would cite. I understand Susannah's impatience with
him. She did not let much of it out when she was here
last month, but I imagine she has a hard time following
him in some of his theories. Surely she has some contrary theories of her own, and I wonder how long she
will let Jeff go off on his current tangent. It is clearly

not only "the birth" that has depressed her, whatever Jeff thinks.

Zada called me last night while I was still puzzling over my being dumped by Yvonne. She was in a depressed state too, wondering why she is in college. All her classmates want to be doctors and lawyers, but Zada only wants to be a housewife. I feel sorry for intelligent shy girls like Zada who are uncertain what to do with their talents. The choices they must make are complicated ones.

There is a danger Zada will become too dependent on me. She has picked me out as a soulmate, and I suppose I am one. I do not mind. In fact, I experience a strange alteration of viewpoint when I talk to her. There is never a question of discussing my own problems, and I would not want there to be. With Zada I must be generous and wise, a solver of problems. I enjoy the role. It is even beginning to come naturally to me.

It is a cold December. The landlord has not seen fit to supply storm windows and has installed a locked box around the thermostat, so there is not much I can do except hang a bag of ice over it when I want the furnace to start up. I have taped the cracks in the window frames, and I often leave the oven on, but I am still cold.

I am thankful I have no car. Jeff used to suffer over his in the winter. I have memories of shoveling and pushing and falling on my face in the snow, and all the time Jeff storming around in a violent temper. Those were the times I liked him least. He was helpless with garage mechanics because he knew absolutely nothing about cars and was convinced he was being taken for a ride. It threatened his self-esteem to such an extent whenever he got his car fixed that he had to come back and pick an argument with me to put himself back in perspective.

Oh, Xavier Fereira, why do you make such allowances for people? You take two steps away from them and act as if you do not care what they do to you as long as you understand their motivations. There are times I feel Lichty is making a mess of my life. He has made me cynical, withheld, and noncommital. Nothing fazes me anymore, and at the same time nothing delights me. Yvonne Morris was nothing when I had her, nothing when I lost her. What kind of therapy is it, putting a stop to feelings?

But then, my feelings have never been what you could call abundant. I was never able to throw myself into a first adolescent love affair, as Jeff was, and now as a consequence I have no memories of innocent romance to get nostalgic over. Jeff has many such memories, and I have always envied them, however foolish they may seem to me now. I would like to recount one of them here because I do not feel like getting back to the story yet.

This is the great romance of Jeff's European year off:

Though he had slept with girls before, or so he would

have me believe, his first real involvement was with a Danish girl named Karen. Throughout our senior year, Jeff continued to carry around a snapshot of her, on a sunny balcony by the sea, wrapped in a white towel, drying her long dark hair. She was very dark for a Dane. I told him she looked like Claudia Cardinale, and he had to agree.

Karen was a bit older than Jeff, but not much. She was, of all things. a dancer in the ballet at the Paris Opera. It is beyond me how Jeff could have fallen for a dancer, but he was only twenty, and if I had been falling in love at that stage of life it might well have been with a dancer too.

Jeff and Karen soon left Paris for Antibes. He still moans about the money he spent on her, the champagne they drank, the expensive hotels they stayed in. This was before Ivy-League Jeff turned into Simple-Living Jeff, before I had exerted any influence on him. Karen inspired Jeff to do things his tight pocket has regretted ever since. I do not suppose the romantic side of it comes into consideration anymore. He has safely filed away the whole episode under the heading, Unwonted Extravagances of the Past.

Karen was off work for a month and must have wanted some excitement, a little travel, someone to follow her around. Perhaps there was more to it than that — Jeff claims there was. She had recently appeared as one of the Bacchantes in a production of *Tannhäuser*, and she performed a modified version of her part for Jeff in a quiet corner of the Tuilleries late one evening and attracted quite a crowd. It was the supreme artistic experience of Jeff's life, or so he said. Perhaps Karen really was a good dancer.

In any case, they were off to the seaside for several weeks. It is rather difficult for untraveled me to write a vivid description of the French Riviera. All I have to go by are the few snapshots Jeff showed me: the aforementioned "After the Bath" shot, one taken by an obliging chambermaid showing the two of them smiling at each other in a grove of palms, and a spectacular shot of a blurry Jeff precariously riding the crest of a wave on a peddle-boat.

Jeff was out of his head with enthusiasm for Karen, but he was making love with her three times a day and could hardly take time to plan a realistic future for the two of them. Besides, the uncertain French they spoke to each other kept them from getting into anything too deep, and, after all, mystical forces were at work, if I am to believe my dreamy ex-roommate. Jeff kept it up for hours when he at last began to confess it all to me. We were sitting around, hot and sticky, in that hole of an apartment. Aztec was still alive and had curled up on my lap. I listened and nodded and sympathized. It was one of the rare times Jeff felt like divulging his private history to me, and I was flattered.

At the end of the month, when Karen had to return to Paris for rehearsals, she found less time for Jeff, indeed very little time at all. It took him no longer than a week to become so jealous of her dancing that she had to tell him she could not waste her energies dealing with his extravagant temper and for him please to go away for a while.

Alone, he took the train south again but did not get off till Florence. He was in a panicky state, operating on the absurd hope that Karen would soon miss him terribly and come flying after him, leaving the Paris Opera behind her forever.

After several dreary days of writing long letters and meandering about the city, Jeff managed to befriend a timid American spinster who was standing beside him in the Uffizi before the huge Leonardo cartoon of the Adoration of the Magi. They went off to lunch together, and the spinster talked about the fears and tensions she experienced while traveling and how they spoiled everything for her. Jeff was soon confessing his own state of nerves, and though he did not at first explain about Karen, his sympathetic companion sensed he had been through something rather crushing and was only too pleased to give him a bottle of her most effective tranquilizers.

Jeff began to calm down somewhat, and during the next few days he told his romantic tale to the kind-hearted woman, both of them subdued by pills and rather oblivious to the goings-on of the beautiful city which neither of them had ever visited before. Jeff still curses himself for having missed so much of Florence.

The comfort offered by the spinster (I have a feeling

her name was Florence too) got Jeff over his panic, but
he found himself growing angry as the days went by
with no word from Karen, and even a little uncomfortable with Florence's constant sympathy which had begun to seem more and more like morbid curiosity. The
grandeur of his romance was being debased by all the
jabber, and Jeff had to put a stop to it.

But Florence was not easily shaken off, and finally
the only thing to be done was for Jeff to get on a train
and go back to Paris. Florence saw him off at the station with tears in her eyes. (She wrote him long, desperate letters throughout senior year, but he never
wrote back.)

When Jeff arrived in Paris, he found himself hoping
he would not run into Karen quite yet and finally had
to admit to himself that he had no true desire to see
her at all. His own version of her remained safe in his
mind, while the real Karen could go on to dance and de-
ceive for all he cared. She was obviously not meant for
him.

So he went on to Amsterdam and did not fall in love
for the rest of the trip.

I must say I enjoyed telling this little tale, but I
seem to be sabotaging the orderly plan of the book. This
chapter was to deal with Jeff and Susannah's wedding.
It does seem odd, after all these pages, that they are not
even married yet. Let me retreat now to that point in
my history, June 1968 (a year and a half ago), when I

dutifully trooped down to Huntington, West Virginia, to be Jeff's best man.

Mr. Kimberk had been having mysterious dizzy spells. He kept having to sit down when he had only been standing up for five minutes, and Mrs. Kimberk was obviously worried. Zada had just graduated from high school, where she had been as wallflowery as Jeff had been popular. Her consolation was that she had made it into Radcliffe, but she had few friends besides another awkward girl named Cathy, and no boyfriends at all. Seeing her brother marry brought her own loneliness to the surface. Her round brown eyes were in tears practically the whole time. Susannah had asked her to be a bridesmaid along with cousin Beth Twombley and Ida Lee, the maid of honor. They made an unharmonious threesome: short, busty Ida Lee, wispy Beth, and Zada blushing and sniffling in her canary-yellow dress carrying a bunch of daisies.

I have to confess that whatever paternal instinct I have emerged for the first time when I saw Zada as a bridesmaid. Our soulmateship dates from that moment. At Christmas we had liked each other, but it was at the wedding we discovered we also understood each other. I say "each other," but perhaps I should just say that I understood her. I doubt that she understood me then and even that she does now.

I could see how she was suffering on Jeff's wedding day, and I went up to her before the service and simply told her I knew she was feeling shaken and not to worry about it, and if she ever wanted to talk to me about it, I would be very glad to.

"Oh, Xavy," she said, choking up a little more, and hesitantly she put her hand on my shoulder. I knew she wanted to give me a hug or at least hold on to me, so I put my arm around her waist, gave her a squeeze, and kissed her cheek. For a moment her hand on my shoulder held me quite tightly.

Then Mrs. Twombley, who did not care for my fuzzy head, came along and hurried me out. I was supposed to be with Jeff and the minister at the front of the church.

I do not know where the impulses came from that made me comfort Zada. When I told Lichty about it, he perked up and has been reminding me of it ever since. I think he runs the risk of making me resist such impulses in the future out of defiance, but perhaps he has a long-range purpose. I find in the course of therapy that just because my doctor and my parents espouse certain attitudes does not mean I might not want to espouse them too.

The Twombleys were quite well off. They lived in a large half-timbered house on a hill by the art museum. I had honestly not known whether to expect a hillbilly cabin or what. I should have realized Huntington would be much like any other city, but it seemed so remote — I could hardly imagine who would live there. Jeff said I was the most provincial of all New Englanders he had ever met.

What struck me most in Huntington was the sky, which never held still. Clouds would collect, turn fierce black, rain a little, then disperse leaving a blue field shortly to be invaded by clouds again, and all this within half an hour. The surrounding mountains must have had something to do with it. It fascinated me, and I spent several hours on the morning of the wedding wandering through the park on the edge of town with my head tilted back watching.

I was treated as somewhat of an oddball in Huntington. But there even Timothy Twombley, Susannah's brother, was regarded as a bit bizarre. Fortunately for him, he played football at Marshall and so was forgiven his appearance which by Boston standards would have been moderate indeed. Jeff was a little too much for them too, but his hair was straight and tended toward the blond and therefore was not as objectionable as mine.

Susannah found it all tremendously amusing. She had always been considered an unpredictable element in her hometown, but her piano playing, like Timothy's football, made up for it.

Mr. Twombley, a barrel-shaped newspaperman, was obviously proud of his nonconformist children, but Mrs. Twombley was a perpetual wreck over the idiosyncracies that kept appearing in them. When I stepped off the plane, she must have said to herself, "Oh, look what Susannah has done now!" Luckily, weddings have a way of making people accept everything in the end.

Until one of your friends gets married, it is hard to envision yourself doing it. My emotions wavered between hopefulness and despair as I thought first, it could happen to me, then, it could not, it could, it could not.

Tom Kimberk, a cousin from Saint Louis, led Mrs. Kimberk down the aisle to sit on the right. Mr. Kimberk followed. Then Timothy Twombley led Mrs. Twombley down the aisle to sit on the left. The organist began the march from *Lohengrin*. Susannah had insisted on the traditional music, despite Jeff's taste for something a little more original, Haydn's "Saint Anthony Chorale" perhaps. Jeff and I followed the bumbly old minister out one side of the altar. There was a slight murmur in the congregation as those relatives who had not yet seen me expressed their dismay.

Zada and Beth came down the aisle side by side. Zada was trembling visibly. Ida Lee followed, her breasts jutting forward as much as ever, and I decided she was a cheap-looking girl and was just as glad I had not tried anything with her, though it would undoubtedly have been fun. Finally, Susannah appeared on her father's arm. She wore her grandmother's wedding dress. The small bones in the family must have passed from mother to daughter, the chunkiness from father to son — quite the opposite of the Kimberks.

I feel I have been guilty of some exaggeration however. I have made much of Susannah's beauty and Zada's plainness. It is my old habit of dividing the female sex into those who excite me and those who do not. But to a cool eye, Susannah was neither extremely beautiful nor was Zada at all unattractive. They both fell within the range of average looks, with Susannah on the prettier end of the scale, Zada on the plainer.

Susannah's fine features went with the delicate lace of her grandmother's dress. Her long red hair set off all the white, and she carried a bouquet, not of flowers, but of plain green leaves. Mr. Twombley looked like a Humpty-Dumpty in his coat and tails as he tilted side to side down the aisle toward us.

Jeff stood beside me in a kind of ecstatic stupor, his eyes blank, his lips drooping, his shoulders slumped, hardly the elated bridegroom. This was the culmination of all his mystical fantasies, and there must have been some regret in that. On the plane coming down, he had been almost unbearable. He would hardly speak and claimed I could never understand what he was going through.

For her parents' sake, Susannah, the atheist, had been willing to put up with an Episcopal service. When the time came, she admitted that for the sake of tradition too she would not have had it any other way. I am sure Jeff, who loved ceremony, would have been only too glad for a Catholic service himself, despite all my horrifying tales of childhood churchgoing. (I used to think to commit adultery was to masturbate and each week had to confess having broken the seventh commandment. The priest never bothered to set me straight.) Jeff's own parents were frankly antireligious, but even Mrs. Kimberk admitted that some remnant of girlhood piety prompted her to wear a hat and gloves in the church.

Jeff had hoped to be able to introduce favorite passages from Keats and Shakespeare into the service, but again Susannah had stopped him. She wanted an ordinary, traditional wedding because, she said, Jeff's tastes changed so and what might be a favorite passage now would surely be disowned a year later. Susannah did not want her wedding subject to revision.

So they simply said the responses as written. I gave Jeff the ring, and he put it on her finger. As simply as that my life fell into a new perspective. I gulped a few times, but Zada could not hold back her tears at all. When the march from *A Midsummer Night's Dream* began, big brother Timothy Twombley stepped up to escort her, Tom Kimberk took Beth Twombley's arm, I took Ida Lee's, and we all followed along after Jeff and Susannah, man and wife, a hard thing for me to realize.

The party afterwards was crowded and loud. Ida Lee elbowed a few hopeful young things out of the way in order to grab the bridal bouquet for herself. The change in my condition did not have a chance to bother me. Only the next day, when I got on a plane for

Boston, alone, did I have to come to terms with my feelings.

Jeff and Susannah went to a little town in Vermont where a business associate of Jeff's father had loaned them his summer house for a few weeks. It was to be a low-budget Kimberk honeymoon. While they were away, my task was to find myself a new place to live.

At the reception I managed to talk to Mr. and Mrs. Kimberk alone and tell them how much good the visit to Dr. Olafsson had done. We were standing on the Twombley's terrace late in the afternoon under that changeable sky. Timothy Twombley, leaning against a tree, was renewing his acquaintance with Ida Lee Sims. Zada looked uncomfortable standing with them trying to be part of their conversation.

"We're very pleased," said Mrs. Kimberk. "It's nice to be able to take some of the credit."

I told her if she ever saw Dr. Olafsson again please to let her know how much Dr. Lichty had accomplished.

When I asked what their summer travel plans were, they said they were returning to Yucatan. "I must see an old Maya friend of mine, Francisco Dzib," said Mr. Kimberk. "I somehow feel with this dizziness of mine I'd better go now. No telling if I'll be up to it next year."

Mrs. Kimberk gave the particulars of her husband's spells, but Mr. Kimberk clearly did not wish to discuss his health, and he returned the conversation to Yucatan and told me about this man Dzib and the observatory at

94

Chichén-Itzá. Zada drifted into the orbit of our conversation, having finally abandoned Timothy to Ida Lee.

"How are you holding up, Zada?" said Mr. Kimberk.

"Okay, Daddy."

"This has been no fun for Zada," he said, putting his arm around her shoulders. "She's been a good sport."

"I'm so glad Xavy's here," she said.

"So are we all," said Mrs. Kimberk.

I was suddenly convinced of how much these three people liked me. Of course, they knew me only as a one-time house guest, and as they had seen nothing of my less admirable side, I had managed to establish a certain positive identity with them. They were probably the only people in the world who interpreted that identity as the actual me. It was the way I hoped all my acquaintances would one day see me, but at least I had these three people to start with. I even felt I could do no wrong in their eyes. They were people I was safe with, who would stand by me. It made me a bit giddy to think of it.

The Kimberks seemed out of place among all the Twombleys. Aside from Jeff's immediate family, only his cousin Tom and the two old aunts, Miss Wilsey and Miss Whalen, had been able to make it. Jeff was annoyed and hurt that Tom's parents, his only real aunt and uncle, had not seen fit to come. "But you know how Kimberks are, Jeff," said his father. "We never went to Adeleine's wedding, did we?" As for Jeff's mother's side, Mrs. Kimberk was an only child and her few remaining relatives had moved out to Palo Alto and never came east.

The Twombleys were another matter. There were Huntington Twombleys, none of them as prominent as the Warren O. Twombleys themselves, but all respectable, polite people, despite their occasionally raised eyebrows. There were Ohio Twombleys and Kentucky Twombleys and even a few mountain Twombleys, what was left of the Appalachian type I had expected to find more widely represented. Uncle Ted Otis was the most notable of these, a crusty old schoolteacher from coal-mining country who cornered me for a full hour to pick my brains and was the only one who did not seem to take exception to my appearance. Then there were the Twombleys' friends, the Twombleys' business associates, the people who worked for the Twombleys, Susannah's old schoolteachers, Susannah's high school pals — in short, the church had been nine-tenths Twombley, the bride's side spilling over into all but the front rows of the groom's.

Mr. and Mrs. Kimberk and Zada and I were thus quite conspicuous standing on the terrace by ourselves. If I had not been with them, perhaps a Twombley or two might have ventured up to make polite conversation, but I scared them off, as cousin Beth explained to me later that evening, tidying up the place after everyone had gone.

Finally, Mrs. Kimberk and Zada were beckoned away by a group of Twombley ladies, leaving Mr. Kimberk and me to ourselves. He suggested we sit down, so we found a spot on the low brick wall which separated the terrace from the well-tended lawn. and he said, "I'm not at ease in a place like this, Xavy, I must confess."

"Nor am I."

"But Susannah's splendid, isn't she!"

"Yes," I said, "at times I really envy Jeff for having latched onto her."

"Ah well, Xavy, you mustn't envy him too much. One can only judge from among one's own romances. Perhaps she wouldn't have been at all the one for you."

I shrugged my shoulders. Surely Mr. Kimberk did not know that Susannah had in fact, however briefly, been one of my romances. I decided to redirect the conversation. "What's happened to your plans to go to Brazil, Mr. Kimberk?"

"That's right, we were all going to go, weren't we? Well, who knows? Perhaps next year, if only the dizziness clears up. You're still game?"

"Of course."

"But I'm afraid this summer it has to be Yucatan. Dzib and I have our project studying the observatory. That's something you should see, Xavy." He put his finger in his ear and shook his head a few times for the dizziness, I supposed.

"Have you noticed the sky here in Huntington?" I said.

"Yes, indeed — it keeps intending to rain, then thinks better of it."

"But have you noticed how fast it moves?" We both looked up. It was nearly evening, and the clouds were rushing by above the twisty branches of the trees in the Twombley's backyard.

After a while Mr. Kimberk said, "What are Jeff's true interests, Xavy? Do you have any idea? He's so disjointed in his enthusiasms."

"I think he's found something in this Roxbury project," I said.

"But don't you find there's something compulsive about it? I used to wander about at his age, conceiving a passion for this or that, but never under the kind of pressure Jeff puts on." He filled his pipe and lit it. "I hope he doesn't tire Susannah out."

"Susannah's used to him," I said.

A waiter in white brought us each a fresh glass of champagne, but Mr. Kimberk let me have his because he said he had had entirely enough. We continued talking pleasantly for a time. He mentioned that I had changed a good deal since Christmas. "You seem much livelier. I know you were quite depressed then, always looking at the floor. We thought you were terribly nice, just wished we could be of more help to you."

Later Miss Wilsey and Miss Whalen came along and joined us on the brick wall. They had been walking through the garden and were full of names of flowers I cannot possibly recall. Then Tom Kimberk appeared, and they told him he really ought to let his hair grow like mine. The two of them wore their peace buttons with aggressive pride, but Tom was a Young Republican and got them into a tedious argument about the war. The old ladies began to lose their control, the gentler Miss Wilsey becoming almost tearful, the enraged Miss Whalen tackling Tom point by point. I slipped away.

Jeff came running up to me when I walked into the kitchen. "Where's the ham?" he said. I was puzzled. "Where's the ham, Xavy? You were supposed to get the ham."

"I was?"

"It's not here. Mrs. Twombley's all in a twit. You were supposed to go down to the grocery store at six thirty and get the ham."

"I completely forgot."

"Oh, Christ!" said Jeff. "It's the least you could do to keep track of a few simple things."

"Why couldn't they deliver it?" I said.

"How should I know? It's been all prepared. Mrs. Twombley wanted you to pick it up. I told you when we were leaving the church. I pointed out the store to you."

"Oh, yes. Well, I'll go now."

"Here, take the keys to Timothy's car." He bolted off through the swinging kitchen door.

Jeff's wedding had really got to him, but I was determined to do my duty as best man and not cross him in anything. I was sure things would fall back into their normal patterns after the honeymoon.

What else is to be said about that day? I did experience one moment of great tension which I have yet to confess. It occurred when we came out of the church and stood on the front steps in the dappled sunlight, shortly before Jeff is reputed to have told me where to pick up the ham. Susannah came over to me, smiled the most mysterious of her smiles, and threw her white-laced arms around me, saying, "Oh, Xavy, sweet old Xavy!" How can I put this delicately? I responded, well, physiologically to her embrace.

5

THIS will be a sadder chapter.

By the time Jeff and Susannah returned from their honeymoon, I had moved out of my red and gold room and found myself the apartment I now occupy, six blocks away. They put Susannah's upright in my old room, and it was there in the shadeless Chinese light that she practiced the rest of the summer.

Jeff finally attacked the kitchen and bathroom with white paint, and together they stripped the maroon wallpaper from the living room walls and painted them tan. You put your jacket on a hanger now instead of tossing it in a corner. You sat straight in your chair and did not put your feet up on things.

It was during the first summer of their marriage that Jeff became disillusioned with his Roxbury project. He felt he was hypocritical going down there supposedly to teach but all the time making sociological guinea pigs of his students. I used to come to dinner every Sunday, and we would all get red in the face talking about the various national dilemmas. I had learned to argue again, and it often took Susannah's playing of Mozart sonatas to calm us down. She played them rather well and should have stuck to Mozart.

It was indeed strange to walk out of my own little place those Sunday evenings and saunter down Somerville Avenue past the gas station and up the creaky stairs that led to my former home, strange to knock on the door, to have no key, strange to be expected to wipe my feet when I came in. Of course, I was grateful for the weekly meal, but it always brought back the same uncomfortable memory, the meal Susannah and I had cooked once over the same stove and served on the same table, which was now set with a cloth, monogrammed silver, and their second-best china.

One evening after dinner, Susannah went into my old room to practice, and Jeff and I sat on the couch with our glasses of iced tea and talked. The fuzzy gray had been replaced with brown corduroy. Nine months ago I had seduced the lady of the house on that very couch, and I mentioned the fact to Jeff.

"I suppose I'm an odd kind of husband," he said, "but it seems pretty funny to me now. Remember her knocking on my door and asking me to drive her home? Xavy, you were a real wolf in those days."

"I wouldn't say that," I said.

"You're settling down more now, though. I can even imagine you getting married."

"Now that you see how easily it can be done," I said.

Jeff let that pass with an indulgent smile and carried forth his argument. "No, but you haven't been taking it seriously so far because you never believed you could get beyond the initial stages. You can believe it more easily now, can't you? Hey, talk about yourself, Fereira. It's been months since I've had to listen to your woes."

"I feel quite detached from you now, Jeff," I said. I gave him what must have been a blank stare. I did not quite know how to explain the way I had come to feel about him.

"You do? Why should you? Don't you think we simply have to adjust to the new setup?"

"We've both changed a lot," I said, "but we aren't going in the same direction anymore. We're really quite far apart now." I was overstressing my new loneliness, still a great one for seeking sympathy.

"I don't find it that way," said Jeff. "It's your misconception about marriage. I think you're more romantic than you accuse me of being."

"Don't give me that," I said.

"But what's more romantic, the happy couple settled into its old everyday routine or the lonely soul wandering about enjoying his torment? It's perfectly obvious. Fereira, you're the most supreme romantic I know." He paused, distracted by Susannah's playing of a Brahms intermezzo in her earnest, unarchitectural style.

"I don't enjoy it," I said.

"But you romanticize everyone's life but your own. That's being romantic."

He was anxious to convince me of this new insight of his, and it became clear he had spent several months thinking me over, trying to fit me into his new scheme of life. He had to figure out a way to protect his marriage from the interloping old pal who might get too much in the habit of appearing at awkward times and hanging about. I must now understand I would always be a guest, welcome when invited, but no longer the permanent fixture I had been throughout their courtship. But this new standard was hard for Jeff's conscience to cope with. He had such fierce convictions about the loyalty of friends and, in reaction to his essential possessiveness, such an obsession with generosity and sharing. He must have figured the dilemma would be solved if I were married too, and so he was trying to encourage me.

As he talked on, I listened and drank my iced tea and did some of my own reevaluating. On one hand, I was a bit amused. There sat Jeffrey Kimberk, hair ever so slightly shorter, clothes just a tad more carefully pressed, talking as his father might have — wise, settled, slowly paced. This Jeffrey Kimberk had once been a source of my social intimidation as a freshman, and yet we were now old friends. As I thought more about it, I became certain that my effect on him had been as great as his on me, and I had the feeling, which I hardly dared admit to myself at the time, that Jeff needed to talk to me as much as I did to him, needed my backing, my understanding. It had never seemed that way before, and I decided our chances for success were rather even at that point. It was a premature decision, but perhaps it was a correct one.

Unfortunately, the evening did not end in such a reflective mood. When we had worn out the discussion of marriage and found ourselves staring into our tea, we managed to stage a real fight. It was entirely pointless. I should have known that Jeff had accumulated certain resentments and suspicions during our months of diminished communication with each other, and if I had only seen Mrs. Kimberk's latest postcard from Yucatan, I would never have allowed myself to get angry with him. His mother had worried him about his father's condition, and that must have made him particularly touchy and prone to fight-picking.

Susannah was now hammering away at the "Waldstein" sonata and did not hear our voices as they grew louder. It was to be the second-to-worst fight of our friendship, the worst having occurred after Jeff ran over the cat.

We were talking about Zada. Jeff began to hint, rather shyly, at the possibility that I might be tempted to use his sister to get me introduced to other Radcliffe

105

freshmen. I put down my glass on the coffee table with a clunk but thought better of getting angry.

When Jeff got no reaction, he pursued the topic. It had even occurred to him, it seemed, that I might do something careless to Zada herself, not physically of course, but perhaps emotionally. He had noticed how much she had taken a liking to me. I still held back my anger and joked how he was awfully obsessed with preserving his sister's virginity. Who was he saving her for?

"Listen, Xavy, I know Zada's no beauty, but she's a really nice girl, and if she would just find some guy who isn't all hung up on sex like a certain former roommate of mine, then she might have a happy time of it, but you just write her off and figure she's not worth anything, and I can see you using her for whatever you can get, and don't say you didn't think of it."

"I didn't think of it, Jeff," I said. "Besides, I wasn't implying Zada would never find a boy friend. I was just kidding you for being so obsessive."

"Dammit, you can say whatever Freudian things you want to about me being a protective brother. I'm not ashamed of it at all. I happen to think Zada's worth protecting."

"So do I," I said.

Jeff leaned toward me, quite red in the face, and said, "Then tell me this, Fereira: why did you give her a kiss before the wedding?"

I was surprised to hear that Zada had told Jeff about

106

that. "Well, why do people usually kiss people?" I said. "Normal people," said Jeff. "But not you. You've said so yourself. Alison, Carol, Darlene, whatever their names were. You admitted you were just out to get something, even with Susannah!"

"You better calm down, Jeff," I said and sat back and glowered at him.

"I've been wanting to get this out for some time," he said.

I reminded him that he had said earlier he just thought it was funny that I had had sex with Susannah.

"Maybe I was being polite."

"Jeff, you're the craziest person I know! What the hell do you have to be polite with me for? Can't we analyze things as they are?"

"All right, Dr. Wichtig, go right ahead. Let's put it all in analytic terms. Let's not do things naturally."

"That's not what I said."

"But that's what you do, you always do. How can I get mad with you? You always make me seem unreasonable."

"You *are* unreasonable, Jeff."

"Dammit, yes! I'm glad I am. What do you know about unreasonableness?"

I stood up and started pacing up and down, and I finally raised my voice because I had lost patience. "You want me to yell at you? What do you want me to say? That I want to seduce your horsy sister? That I want to take Susannah away from you? You're so crazy,

107

Jeff, I can hardly believe it! You're almost paranoid sometimes."

"Don't tell me about paranoia, Fereira! I don't fall into trembling terrors when girls walk out on me. I'm so sick of having neurotic friends. I'm so sick of sitting around listening to their self-centered moanings and groanings."

"I haven't moaned and groaned to you for months. I've grown up some myself, you know."

"Bullshit, you have! Who're you sleeping with now? Who'd you sleep with last month? Who'll you sleep with next month? Who're your friends? What do you do with yourself?" He was standing up too, and we were shouting at each other.

"Cut it out, Jeff. You're no hot shit yourself."

"I don't happen to be paranoid. And don't call my sister horsy!"

"Jeff, it's a fact, she's a little horsy. It doesn't mean I think she . . ." Jeff stepped forward and socked me in the stomach. I said, "Oof!" and turned around and grabbed myself around the waist and collapsed on the couch.

The Beethoven stopped abruptly and Susannah came running in. "What are you two doing? Xavy! Jeff, what did you do?"

"I'm sorry, Xavy," he said.

"Oof, oof," was all I could say. Susannah came over and sat beside me and put her arm around me, and then Jeff came too.

"I'm sorry, Xavy, I didn't mean to hit you at all."

I managed to say, "It's all right."

"You just act so overly rational and unfeeling all the time," he said. "It infuriates me."

I could see he was very much more upset than I had realized. "I know, I know," I said.

"What was it all about? Jeff?" Susannah looked at us both, but neither of us felt like recapitulating the argument. "Jeff, you look awfully red," she said. He was sitting on the arm of the couch beside me. "Jeff, you look lumpy."

"Oh no," he said. He jumped up and ran into the bathroom.

"Is it urticaria?" said Susannah.

"Don't know," I said.

"I'll be right back." She got up and ran after Jeff.

"Oh no!" was all I could hear coming from the bathroom.

Susannah came rushing back. "Where'd you put it, Jeff?"

"Where'd he put what?"

"His adrenalin."

Jeff came in. Now he was gasping, and his face was very red and splotchy. His lips were puffing up and so were his eyelids. He looked quite strange.

"In the end table," he said. Susannah found the spray gun at last, and Jeff inhaled several doses. "I'll be okay. It's just a mild one. I can tell. I'm not having that much trouble breathing. It'll go away." He said everything in gasps.

"You'd better lie down," said Susannah, "and stop talking."

I got up from the couch, still woozy in the groin, and Jeff lay down.

"Don't look at me, Susannah," he said. "It's so ugly."

"No, no, Jeff, it's all right." She was tremendously scared, and it *was* very ugly but not as ugly as I had remembered the attack after the soccer game.

"I shouldn't have got so mad. After all that food. And overheated. It's the worst season of the year for me."

"Shh, don't try to talk, Jeff," said Susannah, kneeling beside the couch and stroking the back of his head.

I sat down in a chair across the room and noticed a picture postcard which had slipped down beside the cushion. It was a scene of Maya ruins which I recognized as the Palace of the Governors.

"Dearest Jeff and Susannah," it said. "We've had to take things quite slowly. Daddy's dizziness is worse. It's such a puzzle of a disease, and I'm terribly worried. How we wish you two were here! I think we'll cut short our stay because we can't really accomplish anything this way and Daddy worries as much as I do, but he doesn't say so. Dzib thinks we should go back too. If we were any other place we would have left long ago, or never come, but Daddy loves it here, you know. You two must be so happy in your newly redecorated home.

Don't let me distress you! But we'll all breathe easier when we're back with Dr. Mundt. Love, Mother." Along one side it said, "Zada seems to be having a lovely time out in Utah with Cathy."

I looked over at the younger Mr. and Mrs. Kimberk. He had his face buried in the brown corduroy cushion and was still saying, "Don't look at me, really, it's so ugly," in a muffled way. She was stroking his hair and saying it was fine.

Finally, Jeff suggested she go play something to calm things down. Susannah told me to watch him and make sure he did not get worse. In a minute we heard her begin the third movement of the "Waldstein" sonata with its sweet tune.

I looked at Jeff's puffy eyes peering over the edge of the cushion. He seemed less red and was breathing more naturally. It was an appropriate time to leave him with his wife. We could sort out the tail end of the argument another day, but for the most part our friendship had been curiously purged.

I went over to him, patted his head, and said, "Thank Susannah for dinner. Everything's okay. I'll see you soon."

I could tell he smiled into the cushion. I snuck out while Susannah was attacking a particularly powerful passage.

When the elder Kimberks returned from Yucatan, Mr. Kimberk went into the hospital for a further round of tests but was discharged with no satisfactory diagnosis made. Then one hot Saturday, he returned from nine holes of golf with a lawyer friend and, sitting down in his rocker to listen to some Schubert, had a fatal heart attack.

It was not Mrs. Kimberk who found him but the neighborhood boy they had hired to mow the lawn. He immediately phoned the golf partner who phoned Dr. Mundt, and when Mrs. Kimberk returned from the public library, where she did volunteer work once a week, Dr. Mundt was there to tell her, as gently as he could.

Jeff called me up, and though he was stunned and largely incoherent, I knew at once what had happened. I said I would be right there and ran out and along the six blocks and cut across the gas station lot. Susannah saw me coming and opened the door as I ran up the stairs. I put my arms around Jeff and then Susannah, and we all stood together for a while and held each other. They were shaken. Neither of them was able to contemplate what had happened. Mrs. Kimberk had called only a few minutes before.

Of course I was also very sad myself. I had lost a secret guardian spirit of mine.

The next day I was in Chicago once more. It was mostly a time for keeping to myself. I was there when Jeff wanted to talk, when Mrs. Kimberk needed diversion, but I knew I should not make them feel they had to keep me entertained, so I took volumes of the complete Shakespeare one by one up to the guest room and read most of the week I was there.

It was the end of August and a terribly hot and sticky time. Some days I took my book and walked the mile to Lake Michigan and lay about in the sun sweating pleasantly, and once Susannah came with me. Jeff thought it would be good for her to get out of the sad house for a few hours. He and Zada stayed and looked through old photo albums with their mother and talked about the times they had spent the summers in northern Michigan when they were little and spring vacations down on Sanibel Island.

Susannah and I probably looked like a young couple to the other people on the beach. We ran down into the water a few times but mostly stayed on our towels and talked quietly. It was strange to lie beside her again, just in our bathing suits, our legs almost touching. Our elbows did touch, and several times she held onto my wrist when we mentioned Jeff's father's death. If sadness had not been hanging over the day, I would have become quite aroused by it all. As it was, I remember waking that night in the midst of a dream of me and Susannah tumbling about on the sand.

"Jeff is so grateful to you, Xavy, for helping out," she said.

"Oh, I feel I don't know what to do for him."

"You're quite good just being here. I think you comfort him more than I do. I'm awkward at it."

"I doubt that, Susannah."

"But it's true," she said and turned on her back.

She had not had much sun that summer and, being

113

a redhead, had to be careful not to burn. I, on the other hand, had spent much of my time down by the river getting brown and looking over the girls, so I did not have to worry.

"Being his wife I have somehow to share the amount of sadness," she said, "but of course it can't go as deep in me because I didn't really know Jeff's father, and yet I get very sad anyway and cry, and I think it offends him because it seems less deep than his sadness, as if I were taking it away from him."

"You mustn't worry about that, Susannah."

"I don't know. He's very unreachable at the moment." She put her hand on my arm. "Let's go into the water. I'm sweating like a pig."

"But a rather shapely pig," I said.

We ran into the water, swam out to the sand bar and back, and splashed around. Susannah was no flirt, but there were moments when she showed a kind of affection which I, on my one track, could only interpret one way.

Zada was quite withdrawn from me that week. She retreated from everyone, except her mother, and I could not be of much help to her.

The news of her father's death had come to her in Utah, where she was spending the summer on a ranch with her friend Cathy. The summer had been a perfect one for her. A couple of ranchhands named Jerry and Earl had paid attention to her, not romantic attention as such, but attention nevertheless, and she had enjoyed

114

learning to ride Western, which was so much more relaxed than English.

And she had made many resolutions concerning her
new life which was to begin at Harvard and Radcliffe in
the fall. She told herself she would speak up in class,
force herself to. She would sit next to interesting-look-
ing people and start friendly conversations. She would
diet, and her mother had promised her a new wardrobe,
and she would at last get rid of her pony tail.

All these things were unimportant when the sad news
came, the phone call from her mother. Zada was called
in from the corral to receive it in the big ranchhouse,
and she sort of collapsed at the seams when she heard
what had happened. Jerry and Earl, and friend Cathy,
and Cathy's parents' friends who owned the ranch did
not know what to do for her but drive her to Salt Lake
City as fast as possible and put her on a plane for home.

I only learned these details this week. Lately, I have
been seeing Zada quite often, trying to help her through
this motivational crisis she is in. It is a bit hypocritical
of me, having dropped out myself, to urge her to stay
in school, but if she can do it, she should.

I usually meet her at the Burger Cottage or the Zum-
Zum for lunch, and sometimes we go to the Fogg Museum afterwards to continue talking. She has told me
many things about her life, and she feels I am the one
who understands her best, more than Jeff, she says. It
is remarkable how well we have come to know each other
these past weeks.

She cried a good deal the week I was in Chicago for the funeral, just as she does now in the stone halls of the Fogg with the medieval Italian paintings around us. She would flop in one of the blue chairs in the front parlor and cry, then walk into the back parlor and sit in her father's rocker and cry some more. She stayed in her room most of the time, but her mother would go in and I could indistinctly hear them comforting each other through the wall of the guest room where I sat reading Shakespeare. It was my resolution to read a play a day while I was there and to continue my project when I returned to Somerville.

There was one time I decided to sit down beside Zada when she was crying and try to comfort her myself. She was sitting on the window seat in the large bay window in the back parlor, watching the rainstorm which was cooling things off a little. There she leaned up against me and I put my arm around her. She held my hand and seemed to fall asleep.

I had some fifteen minutes to adjust to this peaceful posture and try to discover what my feelings were for her. I had never been able to be as big brotherly with my sister Susie or even my little sister Lucy. My family, as much as it yelled and screamed, had never been physically at ease with itself.

I asked Zada this week about that time on the window seat. Had she been asleep? No, she said, but she had daydreamed that I was her father for a time, and then Jerry, her favorite of the two ranch hands out in

Utah (he had danced with her most of the evening at a barn dance). But I was Xavier Fereira unfortunately, I said.

"Not unfortunately," she said, "because you could've been Daddy and Jerry, and Jeff even, at the same time."

"All-purpose me," I said.

After sitting on the window seat for a while, she had finally got up and gone off, and I do not remember on what pretext, but she was gone when Mrs. Kimberk came into the room with a pitcher of lemonade. I was choosing my daily Shakespeare and had decided that *The Tempest* was a sensible choice for a rainy day.

"You read a lot of Shakespeare, Xavy," said Mrs. Kimberk.

"It's my latest project for self-discipline."

"From that edition with the uncut pages, you must think we never read Shakespeare. Our Signets are upstairs on the shelves in my sewing room if you'd prefer them."

I told her the uncut set was fine. I used the letter-opener on the hall table before I began to read.

"Sit a minute, won't you, Xavy, and have a glass of lemonade with me?"

I climbed down from the window seat, which I was standing on to reach the top bookshelf where the Shakespeares were kept, and took a seat opposite Mrs. Kimberk, who handed me a cold glass.

Despite her unhappy preoccupation, I still found it easy to talk to her. At first, I had hesitated picking topics of conversation for fear of hitting on an upsetting one, but it had become clear that she was able to talk about all things and was indeed anxious to do so. So I asked her about Yucatan and if they had come to understand all the subtleties of the observatory before they had to come home.

Unfortunately not entirely, Mrs. Kimberk said. Mr. Kimberk did not have a sufficient knowledge of mathematics to pursue the mystery in all its astronomical implications, but he had been largely satisfied with the start he had made, and so had Dzib.

"This rain puts me in mind of a day at Uxmal," said Mrs. Kimberk as we both looked out at the sheets of rain. "There was a marvelous storm like this when we went there after leaving Chichén, just before we headed home."

She went on to describe the storm, and it seemed to comfort her to recall it. Their bedroom had faced the jungle, she said, and there was a wide balcony on the courtyard side. The balcony was polished tile, and the rain, pouring into the courtyard and into the pool in the courtyard, washed over the tiles and even seeped under the door of their bedroom. From their bedroom they looked out through a lattice shutter across the low jungle, green and thick, pounded by the storm, and in the distance they could see a gray ruin rising above the jungle, the Pyramid of the Magician.

Now in her baggy madras bermudas and puffy blouse, Mrs. Kimberk looked entirely too unadventur-

118

ous and short of breath for me to picture her in such a wild place.

"I'm afraid I must leave you to your Shakespeare now, Xavy," she said. "There are some things I still have to arrange what with the Saint Louis contingent arriving this afternoon." She picked up the lemonade glasses and headed for the kitchen but turned at the door and said, "We might all take a jaunt down there next year, what do you think? I don't want to get feeling bleak about it, as if I could never go back. Better to go back right away, don't you think? Wouldn't it be nice if you could arrange to come with us?"

"It certainly would," I said.

"Philip hoped to get you to Brazil, didn't he, but maybe you'll settle for Yucatan."

These pipe dreams had a way of petering out, but perhaps I may still get to Mexico with Mrs. Kimberk.

The funeral might better be termed a memorial service, or even a memorial concert. The antireligious Kimberks had long before determined the mode of their funerals. There was to be no casket, no minister, no speaking by anyone.

The people filed into the rows of folding wooden chairs in the auditorium of the local public library where weekly chamber concerts and poetry readings were held. It was a plain hall without any religious associations. The walls were hung with portraits of various literary and musical figures prominent when the library was built, most of them quite passé now, except for Mo-

zart and Shakespeare in twin frames hanging on the
wall behind the platform.

On the platform itself sat a string quartet, the play-
ers solemn-faced. Standing lamps provided only dim
light, and there were no candles, no flowers, nothing
which might put you in mind of a church.

As the time for the service approached, Jeff's Aunt
Char walked to the second row on the arm of the rabid-
rightist cousin Tom, her son. They were followed by
cousin Adeleine, a blond with pixie hair, and her husband, some dreary businessman; and finally by Jeff's
youngest cousin Lincoln, fifteen, the only rebellious-
looking member of that family. Then Jeff and Susannah entered the hall, Jeff's arm around her shoulders
and Susannah's tightly around his waist, and they sat
in the front row, and Zada and I sat next to them. Apparently, Uncle Thomas and Aunt Char had assumed
I was Zada's steady boyfriend, and I did not set them
right, knowing their mistake would please Zada.

Mrs. Kimberk was the last to take her seat, escorted
to the front row by her brother-in-law Thomas Kimberk, Senior, even lankier than his older brother Philip
had been, but lacking the moustache and the red-veined
cheeks. Mr. and Mrs. Twombley were there too. They
had flown up from Huntington and would have to return that evening, but they did spend some time alone
with Mrs. Kimberk in the morning, and it had obviously touched her that they had come.

Before the music began, I looked back to see what

faces were familiar. There was a chubby red-haired girl
sitting with her parents whom I took for Cathy. There
was Dr. Mundt and his wife; Mr. Henderson, the golf-
ing partner, and his; and various other professional
sorts whom I had met at the house the day before when
they were paying their respects. And there were some
archaeologists from the University of Chicago, Mr.
Kimberk's most valued acquaintances, but no Francisco Dzib who, with the greatest regret, could not possibly have made the trip. And none of Mrs. Kimberk's
own long-absent relatives from Palo Alto had come.
Miss Wilsey and Miss Whalen were there, of course,
among the many gray heads in the back of the room,
and Jeff said there were people there who had taught
his father in high school. The saddest thing of all was
that Mr. Kimberk had died at only fifty.

When everyone was quiet, the string quartet began
to play. They played without scores and with great re-
straint. It was the slow movement of Beethoven's Quartet in A Minor. Zada found my hand and held it
throughout the playing.

At first, the music made me feel tense and edgy, but
I discovered that it brought me to a clearer plane of
thought. I closed my eyes, sensed only Zada's warm
hand and the music, and with these concentrated sensa-
tions came the image of Jeff's father. I recalled his face
exactly, as if it were to be for the last time.

When the movement was over, I opened my eyes and

121

felt a great sinking in me. That was all there was to the service, and it could not have lasted much more than a quarter hour. The Twombleys had come all that way for a mere snippet of Beethoven. I imagine they were a bit puzzled.

Mrs. Kimberk was wiping her eyes with a white handkerchief held in her black-gloved hand. Though it was hot summer, she had worn gloves.

When we stood to leave, I caught sight of a certain head of a woman among the older people in the back of the room. I had not expected to see her there: Dr. Olafsson. I wanted to get to her and speak to her, but I was nervous about it. I did not know how to approach her or what to say and hoped she would see me and come speak to me first. But she might not even have recognized me. It had been eight months since I had seen her, and she must have seen many faces since then.

I kept my eyes on her as we filed out of the room, but when we were outside I could not find her in the crowd. Then there she was, climbing into the back seat of Dr. Mundt's Oldsmobile and soon spirited away.

Few people spoke to Mrs. Kimberk. Her brother-in-law was sheltering her. She had thanked the musicians before leaving the hall and embraced Jeff and Susannah and Zada, but once outside the four members of the diminished family stepped into their own car, and Jeff drove it slowly away.

I had told Jeff I would walk back to the house, so the family could be alone in the car, and I felt quite alone walking through the shaded streets. I loosened my tie, carried my jacket over my arm, and rolled up my sleeves. It was a terribly sticky day.

I would stay a few more days to help out with things and then be back in my little apartment with no further immediate purposes. This had not been the generative visit the first had been. I felt thrown entirely on my own again.

However, I was pleased to get back to Lichty, and though a mild depression set in, I found myself a step closer to the heart of things. I was more responsive in the office and was able to talk about how I felt about Lichty himself for the first time.

Jeff and Susannah stayed on for another week in Chicago, and one morning I found this letter in my mailbox.

2 September 1968

Dear Xavy,

I guess breast-beating can only be done privately, at least in my household. You were a true help to my mother and to Zada and of course to Susannah and me too. When you left, Zada said she was sorry she hadn't been able really to talk to you, said she was holding herself in the whole time, only was able to express her feelings to you once, she said, when you two were sitting on the window seat in the thunderstorm. She's fond of you. I'm sorrier than ever for my stupidity earlier in the summer (our fight) because I see you've been so good for her, a brotherly kind of closeness I don't seem to be able to supply. You saw how reserved we all are. It must've seemed strange. But Xavy, I think my mother is really down

*low. I don't know what to do. She was always a follower, as
I told you, on their trips to ruins, jungles, digs. She depended
on my father for the lead. What will she do now? You didn't
know how much my mother kept to herself and her family. She
doesn't fit into social life as such. And I can't see her traveling by herself now, though she talks about it. Only now do I
see how much like Zada she is, how dependent on a stronger
person. She even looks more like Zada now. She has her droopy
mouth and sad eyes. What'll ever happen to them? My mother
isn't meant to be a widow at all, she isn't! It's strange to see
what passes on down. I mean my mother's looks and ways to
Zada and ways of my father to me. We're like distillations of
them, as it says in the sonnets, in which they continue, but not
the same, always a new mixture, and crossings of qualities,
gestures, affectations. I have to see myself now as a potential
father, isn't that surprising? I think my father was glad for
me to do things a different way. Of course he held me back
from sillinesses but that was just him being protective. I'd
like not to make a split in my life. I suppose his life seemed
very integrated to you, I don't know. The solid home, the
strong interests, acted upon, followed up. But I often wondered why he never went on to be a real archaeologist. That's
the thing. It's a kind of misery, Xavy, what over-prudent expectations do to a life. We can't just be hobbyists, can we? Or
to be frank, it's all finances! What did my father love most?
His family, music, history, architecture. Why did he have to
be a lawyer? It makes me sad. But it was probably essential
to him. He ordered his life in his own way more than most.
It's just all the money I object to, all the stock holdings. Let
me get off this subject. I hate it. It drives me truly crazy
thinking it over. Susannah and I will be different. I'll have
nothing further to do with the stock market. I have decided to
transfer my entire trust fund either to my mother or to Zada
and have already talked to a lawyer about it (Mr. Hender-*

son). Sounds crazy, you can hit me over the head, but I'm going to do it. My father wouldn't mind at all. Oddly enough he had a lot of faith in me this last year or so, thought what I was doing was terrific. He was remarkable because he truly welcomed the changes his children brought him. What he felt was that death was a clearing of the field for what was new. Not just biologically but spiritually. That's why he hated religion so. I don't want to worry my mother now. She'll understand me, I know. Susannah's perfect. We're entirely of one mind. Do I sound panicky, Xavy? Do you think I'm just taking off on this? I'm very upset. I miss my father terribly much. It's quite late. I came downstairs to think after everyone else fell asleep. And I ended up sitting at his desk to write you, mainly to thank you for coming and being so helpful, but also to sort out thoughts to you. I'll always depend on you, Fereira. This will have to go on. Much to talk about when I get back, long evenings of discussions, and music.

Jeff

18 December 1969

Dear Xavy,

I'm sorry I haven't written for two whole months. It's been a truly bad time. Now it's almost Christmas, and we're going up to my mother's tomorrow to spend two weeks out of this city. Zada's coming home, and I gather she's in some sort of panic too which you probably know more about than I do, but I'll hear all about it, I'm sure. Mother says you've been encouraging her to stay in school. Doesn't sound like the old Fereira.

The only thing that's really fine these days is Philip. He's more wonderful than I ever imagined a baby would be. There isn't a chore connected with him I don't love doing. It's remarkable.

Now as for my career, it seems to be falling in about me. The thing is, Xavy, I just don't have the training to get anywhere in the formal social work business. I'd have to go back to school before I could work my way up. Not that formal social work is what I approve of anyway. But I'm rather use-

126

*less at what I'm doing now. I can't explain it. There's so little
I can do.*

*My mother says to come home and relax for two weeks. You
see I've been operating under such pressure, and Susannah's
been getting upset. Well, you know all about that. She said
you were very helpful when she was there and so was Ida Lee.
It was a good thing for her to get away, didn't you think?
But I guess it goes deeper. I'm afraid I didn't handle it right.*

*She finally came out with some things which have been
bothering her all these months and which she'd been keeping
in to be a helpful wife. No, she doesn't mind us living on not
much to speak of. Yes, she's perfectly happy to make her own
dresses and for me to wear the same jeans every day, all that
sort of thing. It's unimportant. But not in the city, she says.*

*She has an idea of a little, well, even a shack, a hillbilly
cabin, some little place. As long as she has a piano and Philip
can crawl around freely when he gets a little older, maybe in
some sort of artists' colony, not that we're artists, well, she
is, I suppose. Perhaps I am, or could be in some way. But it's
unimportant. She even brought up my trust fund (or rather
my ex-trust fund), and I was just as glad she did because we
hadn't mentioned it and it's always been in our minds even
though we can't draw on it anymore. But she wanted to know
if we couldn't just get enough to tide us over. Philip has
changed a lot of things.*

*Xavy, you'll think I'm a complete turncoat now, but I can't
stop thinking of Susannah and me off in the woods for a while,
up in Wisconsin or the Upper Peninsula (the Porcupine Mountains where my family used to go in the summers), or maybe
even back east, Vermont, New Hampshire. I can't breathe in
this place. I have to take my adrenalin every night before bed
just so I can breathe easily enough to fall asleep.*

You must be chuckling away about how I never seem to

stick in one place. I must give you credit, Fereira, for stick-ing to what you're doing even if it's doing nothing, at least you've stuck to it! How long are you going to? Susannah said she thought you seemed depressed with your lack of progress. But stick to Lichty. It takes time. Couldn't you think of being a teacher for now? You could get a job at some toney private school where you wouldn't need an M.A. and teach rich kids. I wouldn't feel guilty about it. You've just got to get going.

What do you think about Susannah and me giving the woods a try? Of course I haven't made up my mind about it, and I know it sounds drastic. I'm not sure how I could earn my liv-ing up there, maybe I could teach too. I want to get away from everything here. Do you think I have no moral fiber? I can't decide at all. I'd better put this in an envelope and mail it off to you before I re-read it and feel like a fool.

Why don't you look up Ida Lee, Xavy? She's still in that same apartment, but all by herself now with her most recent roommate married off just like Susannah was. You always wanted to get to know her. Susannah says she's very lonely these days, doesn't seem to have any serious admirers. Just a suggestion.

Are you going home for Christmas? Say hello to your fam-ily for me. Mother said you sent her a nice Christmas card. I do have a present for you, but I haven't got around to mail-ing it yet. You'll get it eventually. Better write me at my mother's. I don't think we're going to stick out this apart-ment much longer. I do wish you were going to be out here, especially to see the baby. It was two years ago you were here for Christmas, wasn't it? It was a happier time, it seems.

Don't be puzzled if you don't hear from us for a while. I foresee great tumult until we finally settle where we want to be. But write us.

Jeff

I should have saved this letter for its proper spot in a later chapter, but the chronology of this book was violated long ago, so I have put it here. It arrived this morning, and I knew I would not be able to set about my daily discipline until I had given it some thought. It has puzzled me.

I think the proper course now is to write a letter back saying I knew all along they would end up out of the city, I was just waiting for it to happen, and I'm delighted it is going to. I will say I know their lives will be happier, I know it is the right kind of life to lead, and please make it New England where they stake out their homestead because it would be good to have them around again and I do miss them.

Tomorrow I must go home for Christmas myself. I plan to stay there the rest of the week but have explained to my parents that I have a lot of work to do and will need solitude for it. I have told them almost nothing about my writing, but they are half-convinced I am at last doing something worthwhile and do not want to press their curiosity for fear of discovering they are mistaken. My mother said I could use the attic room and no one would disturb me.

Perhaps going home will not be so painful this time. In the past, my aimlessness has been awkward for me and for them, but now they can take me in smaller doses — I will not simply be hanging around the living room, bored. Besides, there is one big preoccupation at home these days which will keep me in the background whether I like it or not. Robin McPhee, Susie's fiancé, is coming back in February from the war. and they are planning to be married right away. Susie has dutifully sent him a three-page letter every week for two years and has kept her original romantic impulses entirely intact. That strikes me as utterly remarkable.

Other things are changing at home. Mike's wife Linda is pregnant, Lucy is a junior in high school, and my parents are talking about buying a winter place in some awful Florida development. And Tony is at the state college and seems very disappointed that his brother Xavier is not more of a political agitator. He probably feels I have already disappeared over the quickly ascended hill of youth.

I cannot write anymore today. I must go buy Christmas presents for everyone. When I begin the next paragraph, I will not be here in my chilly apartment but in the cozy attic of my parents' house, with its view over the rooftops to the dead river, the sooty abandoned mills, and the black slush that will be everywhere. My parents' house is elevated a bit above it all in a neighborhood where the mill owners once lived, now subdivided for the likes of Alderman Miguel Fereira and family.

Jeff and Susannah returned to Boston ten days after the funeral with no feelings of great hope. Zada flew in with them, exceedingly nervous about the opening of college. She spent the first night at her brother's apartment to give herself twenty-four hours to acclimate herself before facing her dormitory.

Jeff and Susannah took her there the next day. I would have gone along, but I was temporarily employed in a pet shop and could not get off work. It was indeed the most agreeable place I had yet worked. The old gentleman who ran it, Mr. Hatcher, was out of his head and just stumbled around muttering to himself, but he left me alone most of the time, and I had a good time playing with the puppies.

Jeff and Susannah resumed their Roxbury occupations, and everything was as it had been before Mr. Kimberk's death, except Zada was now nearby in Cambridge and always joined us for Sunday evening meals. Her resolutions to contrive a new image for herself had been forgotten. Her pony tail remained, her wardrobe was unchanged, and she was even more retiring than before.

Susannah had promised her mother-in-law to take Zada to one of the stylish shops in the Square and see to it she got outfitted, but whenever she suggested it, Zada could not find time. She had so many books to buy and read and papers to write and she was already behind schedule. Besides, the damage had been done. She had already made an unstylish impression on her dormitory mates and on all the boys in her classes.

Throughout the fall of 1968, I looked forward to the Sunday dinners more than anything else in my rather unspectacular week (except perhaps my Lichty appointment). The three-cornered friendship had finally struck its most comfortable stride. It seemed the days of quibbles and squabbles were past, and we could claim to have reached our maturity.

I now see that period as the end of our lingering attachment to student ways rather than the beginning of adulthood, for we still had made no particular commitments beyond those of students and were all more doubtful than ever about our careers. Jeff was becoming increasingly depressed by his insignificant project and disturbed over its moral validity. Susannah had all but given up the dream of becoming a concert pianist and no longer pretended to be working things up for contests or recitals but played just for herself. And I, having for a time convinced myself that finding homes for fat little puppies was a humane thing to be doing with my life, began to realize I was wasting my time as usual, and I eventually quit the job.

Jeff and Susannah went to Chicago at Christmas, and though Jeff had told me nothing about it, he was hoping to investigate the possibility of doing work on the West Side which might prove more rewarding than his work in Roxbury. Several of his old high school friends were working on the West Side, and they made it sound very exciting. Jeff decided to make the move almost immediately after talking to them. Susannah seemed perfectly agreeable, and by the time she and Jeff returned to Somerville, the whole thing was arranged and it was merely a matter of subletting their apartment, renting a U-Haul trailer, and moving out.

I had had no premonition that such a thing would happen. I had somehow been envisioning Susannah, Jeff and me growing old down the street from each other. The proposed move to Chicago would be much more disruptive to the pattern of my existence than their marriage had been. All at once I was to be entirely deprived of my best friends' company, a thing my otherwise isolated soul depended on. Zada was upset too because her brother's proximity had been a comfort to her at college, but like a good sport she tried to pretend it was all for the best, and I suppose I did too.

I will conclude this chapter with a reconstruction of the day Jeff and Susannah moved out.

I woke up in my own apartment and looked at the walls. I had not made any effort at redecoration and had only recently stuck up some National Geographic maps, which Jeff had been about to throw away, to cover the worst stretches of cracked plaster. I must have depleted my creative energies doing my Chinese room in the old place, for I felt no impulse to do a thing to the new one. Only my brass bed gave character to the room.

My apartment was cold. I sat up in bed and creaked my bones a bit and then reached across the duskiness and flipped up the windowshade. The bright light sent me under the covers for a while longer, but then I remembered I had to get up. I was supposed to help Jeff and Susannah load their trailer.

I stumbled about the place in the longjohns I resorted to in the winter and fixed a cup of tea and some waffles from the batter I had foresightedly made the night before. I tried not to think of what was about to happen, interpreting my uncomfortable feelings as dread of all the physical labor lying before me that morning. Of course I was dreading a much greater thing. I had not begun to contemplate what my life would be like without my old pals.

I sat eating for some time. One waffle after another puffed up inside my waffle iron, and memories which I did not wish to dwell on kept bothering me. Finally, one dominated the others — the memory of Susannah's first evening in the apartment she was now vacating. As I cleaned off my plate and put the syrup back in the cupboard, I thought of it; as I scrubbed myself in the shower, I thought of it still; getting dressed, I could not stop thinking of it; and all the way down Somerville Avenue in the winter morning air, I remembered Susannah and me lying together in bed and tried to estimate how much she might have been attracted to me at the time and what could have happened if I had acted differently.

Jeff and Susannah were at breakfast when I arrived and were amazed to see me up so early. They themselves had overslept, and Susannah was still in her pink bathrobe. I had a sausage or two and a piece of coffee cake, and then Jeff and I took Spritely to pick up the U-Haul.

As Jeff signed the various forms and handed over the cash, I strolled along the row of orange and silver trailers and thought how it might feel to be moving somewhere myself.

Jeff had enough difficulty in traffic without also maneuvering a trailer, and that day his nerves were precariously balanced anyway. I always used to think Jeff had a great resource of internal calm, the product of understanding parents and other such suburban comforts, but I was quite wrong. For reasons I cannot possibly discover, he has deep pits of fear and doubt and loneliness in him, and the more I became aware of them, the less he intimidated me. In recent weeks (and particularly after receiving the letter that begins this chapter), I have found myself worrying seriously about him for the first time in the course of our friendship.

"I don't see how I'll ever make it to Chicago with this thing," he said.

"It'll be easier on the pike," I said.

"Shit, I'll be glad to get away from the way people drive around here."

He was hunched up at the wheel, nervously glancing left and right and twiddling his fingers on the wheel. He wore an army parka with a long green and white scarf flung casually around his neck. His jeans and engineer boots were covered with gray slush. A car had splashed him as we were walking from the car to the U-Haul office.

Someone pulled out suddenly in front of us, and Jeff slammed the brakes and let out a series of grossities.

"Calm down, Jeffrey, you'll never make it through the day," I said.

"I'm really nervous," he said. "I'm sure we're doing the right thing, moving, but it's no breeze. I won't feel right until we've got everything safe in its new place."

He had great difficulty parking the trailer in front of the building. I got out and tried to direct him but only annoyed him further. When we got upstairs, Susannah, now in jeans and a shirt stained with tan paint, made us sit down and collect ourselves before beginning the tedious task before us.

Jeff had made three lists. One listed everything that had to go: books, records, the most valuable wedding presents, certain pieces of furniture and clothing. The second listed, in order of priority, the items which were not absolutely indispensable but which Jeff would like to take along if he could. And the third listed everything that was to be abandoned, with X's by the things to be given to Xavy. I do not know why Jeff bothered with the third list, but he liked to be comprehensive.

Susannah had made certain revisions. She had insisted that Jeff's wicker chair be abandoned, and he had consented reluctantly though he loved the ugly thing. Her own sacrifice had been the piano. It had been sold to a music student in the Back Bay and had already been trundled away. But she would get a better one in Chicago. Her parents had promised to finance it.

I sat on the couch, which was fuzzy gray again and was being left for the new tenants as an added attraction (the corduroy slipcovers had been salvaged first). The walls were now bare, but here and there were little stickum patches that Susannah had not yet washed off.

Jeff's plan was for Susannah to do the light cleaning while he and I loaded the trailer. Then all three of us would give the empty apartment a thorough going-over as a courtesy to the serious-faced Indian couple from Madras who were moving in, and finally we would carry all the hand-me-downs over to my apartment and Zada would join us for lunch. I had volunteered the lunch to ease matters for Susannah, but she was taking the whole affair quite calmly and only got the giggles now and then over Jeff's frantic behavior.

"Well, let's get at it," said Jeff. He unfolded the first list and pointed out the boxes and piles that had to go first.

"Don't overdo it, Jeff," said Susannah. "Remember your urticaria, and this is an emotional strain too, and you know how you might react."

"Onion-sauce, onion-sauce," said Jeff as he picked up three cartons at once and puffed down the stairs with them.

I was more moderate in my efforts. When I am alone and have a physical task before me, I find myself capable of surprising feats of endurance, but when I must work in conjunction with others, the old lack of confidence asserts itself and I find myself carrying tidy little loads, holding up the easiest corners of things, and letting everyone pass me by in their zeal to get the job done. It is an absurd way for me to be — I am perfectly capable of doing a respectable amount of hard labor.

In tribute to the solemnity of the breaking-up of my friends' home, I wish I could recall here each load I carried down the stairs that day. Each made me more depressed, and each time I climbed back up the stairs and stepped into the apartment, it was emptier and Susannah had cleaned away a little more of the traces of their having lived there.

As the U-Haul filled up, Jeff's temper quickened. Now came the tricky business of seeing how far down List Two he could get. Of course, he would have liked to have taken everything he owned, but the cost of renting a larger trailer prohibited it. There was no chance of finding room for the wicker chair, but unfortunately the bookcase which I had hoped would be left for me slid in flat on top of everything, much to Jeff's satisfaction. I felt ashamed for wishing it would not. I had been trying to comfort myself with thoughts of what I might inherit after the move.

After everything was loaded, Jeff decided he could get more in if he just rearranged a few things at the bottom. I told him he was crazy and left him to deal with it by himself. I was worn out and cold, and besides it was a good opportunity to be alone with Susannah for a few minutes — not that I had anything particular to say to her, but I wanted to have an undistracted moment with her nevertheless.

When I came in, she was at the window looking down at Jeff and the trailer. "What's he doing now, Xavy?" she said as I flopped on the old couch for the last time.

"Rearranging everything."

She threw up the window and leaned out. "Jeffrey Kimberk! Are you out of your head? Put that all back and come up here and relax!"

"I will in a minute. I think I can get the red barrel in if I fit it over the lamp under the coffee table."

"We don't want that old barrel anyway," said Susannah.

"Calm down, calm down, I'll be up in a short while."

Susannah let the window fall. Its ropes were broken, and the panes rattled when the window slammed. "I'll be glad when we're at last on the road," she said, and came and sat next to me on the couch.

"I guess *I* won't be," I said, giving her blue-jeaned thigh a pat.

"Oh, Xavy, we'll miss you, I haven't really said so yet. We'll miss you most of all, you don't know how much."

"I'm sure you will," I said.

"Oh, I will, I will, Xavy, I will."

She leaned back and looked suddenly glum and took hold of my hand and rested her head on my shoulder. I patted her long red hair which fell against my chest.

139

"Why should I be so depressed about moving, Xavy?"

"Are you depressed?"

"Very, very depressed. I haven't been so depressed since the day after Jeff asked me to marry him. Remember that?"

She looked up at me, and I nodded.

"It'll be all right when you get there," I said.

"I really don't want to move, Xavy. I've been happy here. I could stay here for years happily."

"You're being good about it though," I said.

"Oh poop," said Susannah.

"What sort of talk is that?"

"Poop, poop, poop. It's what I feel like." She got the giggles for a moment.

"Susannah, good heavens."

"You know what I was doing when I was packing the books last night?" She got the giggles again. "I was putting poop into the title of each book I packed." More giggling. "I was in complete hysterics. *The Poop Also Rises, Seize the Poop, Tender is the Poop, Pale Poop, Wuthering Poops!*" Susannah began to shake with the giggles. "*Bleak Poop, Our Mutual Poop,*" she managed to splutter out in gasps. "Huxley was the best of all," she said, trying to calm herself down.

"Susannah, whatever are you talking about?"

"Listen — *Poop Yellow, Antic Poop, Brave New Poop, Poop and Essence, After Many a Poop Dies the*

Swan, Poopless in Gaza, Those Barren Poops, Poop Counter Poop . . ."

"Susannah, are you off your beam?" But I had to admit it was funny.

"Or George Eliot — *The Poop on the Floss, Middle-poop . . .*" She was bouncing about giggling, and tears were coming into her eyes.

Jeff appeared at the door with the red barrel over his shoulder.

"Or more Dickens," said Susannah. "*The Old Curiosity Poop, Poop Twist, Hard Poops!* Every time I think of it . . ."

"Susannah, it really isn't funny anymore," said Jeff. "Want a barrel, Xavy?"

I said no thanks.

"Mr. and Mrs. Nilakantha win the barrel, then." He set it in the corner it had previously occupied and put the cattails back in it.

"*Poop the Obscure! Far from the Madding Poop!*"

"Susannah, it isn't funny," said Jeff.

"*Poop and Prejudice!*"

"Susannah!"

"*Across the River and Into the Poop! To Poop and Poop Not!*"

"Susannah, if you don't cut it out I'm going to have to strap you down."

"But I didn't do Hemingway last night. *The Green Poops of Africa!*"

Jeff looked at me and shook his head. I was chuckling.

"*Poop in the Afternoon!*" said Susannah holding her stomach and gasping for breath, her cheeks running with tears. "*A Moveable Poop!*"

"All right, that did it," said Jeff. He reached down and picked her up under her knees and around her shoulders and she squealed, and he held her high in his arms and spun around with her in circles until they were both so dizzy they staggered to a stop and collapsed on the floor. "That's the treatment." said Jeff trying to catch his breath, "every time you do another one."

"Everything's spinning," said Susannah. "Xavy keeps going by."

The two of them lay on their backs and were silent for a while.

"I have two of the goofiest friends," I said.

Next on the schedule was the big cleaning (Jeff had a fourth list of everything else that had to be done and in what order). Every windowpane had to be degrimed, the tops of all the doorframes dusted off. That was Susannah's assignment. I was issued a bottle of ammonia and a sponge and directed to scrub all porcelain surfaces to a shine. And Jeff went downstairs to borrow a vacuum cleaner from the people who lived below and soon was whirring up and down the hall and around corners muttering under his breath everytime he had to stop the thing and change attachments and shouting "Fuck!" whenever the cord got tangled around something.

When Susannah finished the windows and the high dusting and had washed all the stickum off the walls, she started climbing about the kitchen, wiping shelves and lining drawers with fresh newspaper, determined to impress the Indians. From time to time she got the giggles again but never yielded to the temptation to let us in on the book title she had just inserted "poop" into.

Jeff and I set about waxing the floors, the finishing touch. Unaccustomed to such protracted physical exertion, I was aching and panting and feeling quite inadequate and down on myself, but at last we finished, and Susannah was pleased with us.

It was almost noon, and I was worried that Zada was already waiting for us at my building, so I suggested we go have lunch. Jeff pulled out List Three, and the three of us managed between us to carry all the things I had decided were worth salvaging. It was a considerable haul — a few records, some unglued paperbacks, a carton of half-empty jelly jars (Jeff was a connoisseur of obscure jellies), leaking sacks of sugar and flour, cake mixes, Worcestershire sauce, a steam iron, a wobbly card table, a lamp made of a Grand Marnier bottle, a tie rack, and much more. As we staggered outside, we passed Jeff and Susannah's conjugal mattress dumped by the garbage because they had discovered it was infested with some sort of black bug.

Zada was peering out the vestibule of my building. She opened the door for us and took the records that were slipping out from under my arm. I put the whole load down, and the books balancing on the jelly carton slid all over the floor. I had to try five pockets before I found my keys, but in a few minutes the frustrations of the morning had been forgotten and we were warm and relaxed in my bare little apartment eating hot dogs and drinking a farewell bottle of Mateus.

"Save a little of that wine," said Jeff. "There's a ceremony I have to perform with it back at the apartment."

"What's that?" said Susannah.

"You'll see. It's an old custom when you leave a place. That girl I told you about, Karen, used to do it."

"Ah, the fatal Karen!" said Susannah tousling Jeff's hair. It seemed she knew something of his extravagant past.

We were all sitting on the bed — there was no other place to sit except the rickety chair in my kitchenette. Susannah was leaning against Jeff who was leaning against the head of the bed, and she had her feet propped up on my knees. I was leaning against the foot, rather uncomfortably, and Zada had her shoes off and her feet up under her and was leaning in my direction on her left arm. She had dripped ketchup on the sheet and had covered it up with her skirt hoping I would not notice, as if such a thing would have mattered to me.

As with all conversations at times of parting, whatever we had to say only detracted from our private thoughts. Luckily, we could not draw it out for long. Jeff planned to make it to Herkimer, New York, before

144

dark. Susannah had a friend from music school who taught piano there and would put them up. Then it would be on to Chicago in one long day.

Zada and I washed up the few dishes while Jeff and Susannah spoke quietly to each other on the bed. Then Jeff took what remained of the wine, and we all strolled for the last time together down Somerville Avenue to the old place.

Attributing my rumbling stomach to the three hot dogs I had just consumed, I concentrated my thoughts on the odd fact that the steps I was taking still led to a place where I felt at home, but later in the afternoon the same steps, taken in the same direction, would not. The place would echo with Hindi and smell of curry, or so I imagined it would.

We climbed the stairs in single file, and Zada and I wondered if we should even be there at such a moment. It was no longer a matter of a few hours but of a single hurried minute, just a spill of wine on the floor (that was Jeff's ceremony — he had even thought to tell the Nilakanthas about it, so they would not be disturbed by the puddle), and they would set off.

The memory that had troubled me in the early morning returned. I poked my head into what had once been my own room, still red and gold with the black floor and gold ceiling. I would never see it again, and I had as many things to say good-bye to there as Jeff and Susannah had.

I heard the splashing of the wine and turned around.

145

Jeff nodded at me with satisfaction from the middle of the empty living room. Behind him, the spotless windowpanes were shining with sunlight. Then Susannah took his hand, and we all left the apartment in silence.

Outside, I gave Susannah a hug and Jeff a pat on the back. Susannah hugged Zada, but Jeff just gave her a little poke in the stomach before he got into the car. Susannah went around to the other side and got in. Jeff rolled down his window, and I leaned over to say goodbye once more. Susannah had her arm around his shoulders. The two of them looked out at me with smiles, and I stood up when Jeff started the car.

"This thing'd better get us there," he said.

"You'll get there," I said.

"Good luck, Fereira."

Jeff rolled the window back up, we all waved, and they drove away.

I do not wish to recall the feelings I had at that moment, so I will end the chapter here.

7

I am disappointed with all I have written so far, ashamed of the way I appear in it, and impatient with the way I still seem to be. I had hoped to be able to portray some progress in my character by this point, but I cannot discover any, no matter how I sort things out. And I still have the worst to tell.

I do not know if I can string this thing out much longer, and I certainly do not feel able to resolve all the conflicts I have set up. I had a suspicion when I started that I would get into the book and then find myself with nowhere to take it in the end. But I ignored the suspicion and plunged ahead with a faith that the answers lay in the writing itself, that I would be forced to resolve matters in my life for the sake of the book, if for nothing else.

But the book has depressed me and only made me feel more sharply how I have wasted these years. I am a waste, and surely this book, which I have been writing mainly as a delaying tactic, is a waste too.

Perhaps it was my visit home last week that depressed me so. My parents' cautious hopefulness for my mysterious project may have turned me from it. I have always responded negatively to their encouragement.

It was a desperate and lonesome time for me after Jeff and Susannah moved to Chicago. I was quite well defended against a recurrence of my panic attacks, but I did feel bleak and spiritless, and Lichty had me coming in three times a week for a while.

In January there was a false spring, and I spent my time walking about sadly through the streets and in the parks. Despite my low mood, I found myself enjoying the exercise and decided to begin a new self-disciplinary program of physical improvement. I bought a chinning bar and established a healthier diet, lots of raw vegetables and fruit juices. I also revived my Shakespeare project, which had fallen apart over the fall, and made up an ambitious list, as Jeff might have done, of the one hundred books I intended to read in 1969.

But for all these new regimes, I was in low spirits most of the time, and I confess the most exciting moment of the day was when I checked the mailbox to see if anything had come from Jeff and Susannah.

I got one long letter right away describing their new place in Chicago, but it was not until Groundhog Day that I heard from them again, and then it was only a birthday card. At the bottom it said, "Guess what, Xavy! We just found out Susannah is going to have a baby! Due in late September." That was all.

I saw little of anyone. Zada was deep in her studies and taking them very seriously. She was worse than Jeff had ever been. Her sophomore year has been no better. In fact, I am to meet her at the airport this afternoon. She is flying back from Chicago early because she has three term papers due and needs plenty of time to work on them. She allows herself no respite, one week of vacation and then back to work. Perhaps she is piling it on, hoping she will break down under the strain and not have to go on. That is what I did.

Oh, I cannot write anymore today.

After I stopped writing yesterday afternoon, I wrapped myself in my various cocoons and sloshed my way to the Square. There I bought a copy of *The Confessions of Felix Krull* (I am way behind on the hundred books, and 1970 is almost here) and descended into the subway, which with three changes of line conveyed me to the airport.

I was much too early for the plane and managed to read all of Book One, at times laughing out loud and provoking smiles on the other faces sitting about the waiting room.

At last, Zada's plane taxied to the gate, and she came down the steps in the midst of a holiday crowd and across the oily concrete to the door where I stood waiting. She carried a bulging bookbag on one arm and a big purse slung over her shoulder and was warmly wrapped in her bearish coat and the scarf I had once given her.

She looked relieved when she saw me and said, "I was afraid you wouldn't still be here," in her chortly voice.

"Well, I am," I said and put my arm on her shoulder and kissed her cheek.

Both her cheeks turned red with pleased embarrassment. "We were in a holding pattern," she said.

I took the bookbag and we pressed through the people, along the corridor, and to the front of the luggage-claim room, and I asked her how everyone was at home.

"Mother's a little low. But she's taking a history course at Northwestern."

"How's your nephew?"

"Oh, I brought you some more pictures. He's adorable. He loved the Humpty you sent."

"Does he do much yet?"

"No, no, just makes a lot of burping noises."

"And Jeff and Susannah?"

"Oh, I don't know. Susannah's very quiet. Jeff says they have to relax for a while. They don't know what they're going to do at all."

Zada saw her large green suitcase slide down the rack, and soon I was struggling with it out to the bus stop.

"How about you? Have you calmed down at all?" I said.

"I promised myself I wasn't going to bother you with my fits anymore," Zada said.

It was already dark, and the lights of the airport were spattered about in shiny wet patches on the roadway.

"How about you?" Zada said after a quiet minute.

I told her that my Christmas visit home had been somewhat tedious and that I was fast losing interest in my book and suddenly a tremendous impatience had taken hold of me.

The airport bus came soon and took us to the subway. I had difficulty lifting the suitcase over the turnstile. A year of chin-ups has not done much for me — I seem doomed to runtiness.

Forty-five minutes later, we reached Zada's dormitory, the suitcase having traveled the last few blocks precariously balanced on my head. The head resident, a stern young woman, let us in and nodded her reluctant approval when Zada introduced me as "Xavier Fereira, a friend of my brother's."

The dormitory was deserted. Zada had had to get special permission to return early from vacation. I slid the suitcase down the freshly waxed halls to her room, leaving a dramatic scar. I had never been to Zada's room before. There were Franz Marc horses over the bed and Géricault's "Racing at Epsom" over the desk, and the bookshelves were full of the library books for

her term papers — the Italian Renaissance, Dostoev-
sky, Primate Behavior. I thought of my own miserable
sophomore year.

"Zada, how can you face sitting up here for a week
all alone with these books?"

"You don't know what trouble I went through to get
those books," she said. "They're due in a week. If I
don't use them now, I'd never get them again. Everybody's trying to get them."

"But Zada, you take it too seriously."

"What else am I going to do? It takes me a week to
write one paper, let alone three." Her voice had a nervous tremble in it, and I already sensed the panic which
she had promised herself not to bother me with.

I unbuttoned my jacket and took off my earband and
the gloves Jeff had sent me for Christmas. Zada was
hanging up her coat in the closet.

"Wait a minute," I said. "You certainly aren't going to start right now. Why don't I take you out to
dinner?"

When she turned around in the closet, she was sniffling. "Xavy, I hate college so much. There's no point
in being here. I don't think I can stand it anymore. It's
as simple as that. What am I going to do? I can't face
writing those papers."

She sat down on the edge of her bed and squinted her
round eyes, but the tears were already coming out. I
came and sat beside her and let her cry and go on talking against my chest.

"What's ever going to happen? I'm so depressed about things. Every time I think I might do something, I realize I can't really do anything. Oh, and I wasn't going to bother you with all this. I went on and on to my mother too. It wasn't fair of me. And Jeff was so low. It upset me so much to see him. I've never seen him like that. And here they've got a brand-new baby. I feel like everything's a mess. Those papers! Primate Behavior. It's so ridiculous. I feel like such a stupe bothering you with it all. You must've been so glad when I left for home to get rid of me for a week. All I ever do is act this way when I'm with you."

"No, Zada, don't apologize for being upset. That's the last thing you should apologize for."

"But for bothering you with it. There's no reason you should have to listen to it. You've got your own problems. I really don't know why I get so wrought up. It isn't any one thing. I'm always this way lately, on the verge of tears."

"There's nothing I can say to make things better," I said.

"I know."

"But don't you think the best thing now would be for us to go out to dinner and some stupid movie and forget the papers for tonight?"

"That'd just make it worse, Xavy," she said, as if she were angry with me for suggesting it. She was wiping her eyes and sniffling.

"But you're too upset to get any work done."

153

"I know, but I have to anyway."

"What if I volunteer to help you take notes and type them up?"

"No, no, you can't do that."

"Why not?"

"I've got to do it. You can't do it."

"You'd let me help you."

"You can't be helping me write term papers. You've got your novel to work on."

"Oh Zada, I'm just wasting my time as usual. I've got plenty of time to help you. I told you how impatient I was with it anyway. It isn't working out. I probably won't finish it."

She had stopped crying and was sitting up straight looking at me. "Can I read it?"

"No, it's not meant to be read by anyone. It's not a novel. It's just my ramblings."

"Please, I want to, Xavy."

"No, it's not the sort of thing I can let anyone else read. It really isn't, Zada. If it was, I'd be glad to let you. I don't know why I'm doing it anyway. Come on, aren't you hungry? Let's go out and eat."

"They fed us on the plane," she said, but then she got up and wiped her eyes with her scarf and looked at herself in the mirror over her dresser.

I did not say anything but let her collect herself. When she had pulled her coat back out of the closet and put it on, we walked down the hall and out into the cold air without saying anything for some time.

154

She cheered up at dinner, and I amused her with tales of my brothers and sisters, and of my parents, and the awful years at prep school and then at college when I was her age. She found it hard to believe I had ever been such a clod.

This week I have been helping Zada and have not worked on this book. Wednesday night, I celebrated the turn of the decade by taking her to a rerun of *Black Orpheus*, and now she is rattling along on her papers.

It is a social form I have never given myself the pleasure of partaking in before, going out with a girl without feeling the pressure to get somewhere with her. But in a way it is unfortunate that I am not more attracted to Zada because I like her in most other ways. I do fear that my unromantic friendliness may be difficult for her to deal with, but perhaps it is only another outrageous presumption of mine to assume she has any romantic thoughts about me at all.

I must reiterate that I am growing quite impatient with this book. All week I have told myself I simply needed a week off and will get back to the business of writing next week, but I am acquainted with my behavior patterns — when discipline breaks down in me, it breaks all at once, to avoid drawing out the painful process. I do not think there will be much more of this book.

The material I have to deal with in this seventh chapter is dreary anyway, for it is somewhat shameful to admit that my unmotivated way of living, which might have been barely forgivable in 1968, stretched across 1969 as well. There is very little of my own to report, only the occasional letters from Jeff, musings in the Kimberk manner, telling of the progress of his project and Susannah's pregnancy and finally of the birth of Philip late in September.

As with all my little projects, I have tuckered out on this one after a mere six or seven weeks of well-intended application. Ever since I first broke from overstudiousness some five years ago, I have been unable to call back the faculty of patience which once enabled me to plod along, as if under some great intimidation, and to get things done.

I must ask Lichty if there is such a thing as a healthy variety of that intimidation and how I can impose it on myself, but I know what his answer will be: "How do *you* think you can, Mr. Fereira?"

I might well have left the book at this point, for I closed my notebook, put on a jacket over my sweaters, and strolled out into the cold, down Somerville Avenue past the old place and across the tracks toward the Square. But I began to feel bad having left the book where it was, as if I had a responsibility to it, inanimate object that it is, to account for a few more things.

Then I admitted to myself why I have come to a halt — it is because I am approaching the scene I have dreaded most. I may rationalize that I cannot bear to drag through an account of another stalemated year, but it is the event at the end of the year that is really unbearable. Unless I force myself otherwise, I am very likely to leave the book dangling right here simply to avoid having to confess it at all.

So as I was walking, I turned around, stopped in a corner grocery to warm up, and then ran most of the way back to my apartment (slipping on a patch of ice and banging both knees), and here I am again holding the pen.

I must force myself to skip ahead to the final scene now, if only to punish myself with it one last time. And then when I stop writing today I will not have to get back to it, not next week nor ever again, and further-more, I doubt that I will even want to *think* about the Kimberk complex for some time to come.

Eight weeks ago in the beginning of November, I was lying here in my bed in this dim apartment anticipat-ing a visit later in the day from Yvonne Morris, whom I had just met and invited over for the afternoon. The casual sort of thing I was getting myself into went against my therapy, and I knew it was more of my stubborn holding on to my old unsatisfying ways, but I would get into it anyway.

When I heard a tap on my door, I jumped out of bed and tripped over the cord to my telephone, which fell off the end of the bed onto the floor, and there was a female giggle on the other side of the door. I pulled on a pair of jeans, figuring it must be later than I thought if she was here already.

I opened the door and, shading my eyes, blinked out into the bright vestibule expecting to see Yvonne Morris, but it was Susannah. She had come for her restorative visit.

I began to shake, I was so surprised and glad to see her. She was glad too and hugged me once and then again, and we both jumped about happily until we calmed down a bit and could look each other over seriously. I saw that her eyelids kept blinking to discourage tears and that she kept stretching her fingers as though she had cramps in them. It worried me to look at her, but I hugged her a third time and practically danced her into the room.

Her hair was even longer than it had been, but it looked wispier and browner and her face looked gray. She wore a battered brown coat, which she took off, and beneath it one of her homemade Indian dresses.

"What's all this?" she said, pointing at the rumply bed and the drawn shades.

"Oh, that's just me oversleeping. What time is it?"

She did not know. "I probably should have called first, Xavy."

"No, no," I said. "It doesn't matter. I'm so glad to see you. I didn't know when you'd be coming. When did you get here?"

"Yesterday morning. I should've come to see you yesterday."

"Dammit, you should've come right away!"

I kept holding her hands and looking at her. There were things about her I had forgotten in nine months, that we were the same height (I had been thinking of her as taller), the sort of stubby fingernails she had for playing the piano, how quiet her voice was.

"I've been with Ida Lee pulling myself together," she said, bowing her head as if in apology, looking at the floor.

"I hope she's been a help."

"She has, but she has her difficulties too."

"I hope you'll tell me about everything, Susannah."

"If you want me to. Oh, but I don't want to think about it, Xavy. I just want to see you and mumble around with you again."

"I'm always good for that," I said.

I suggested we have some tea. Susannah smoothed out the bedclothes and sat down, and I brought her a cup and sat down with a cup of my own on the bed, but carefully apart from her. I was feeling oddly asexual, probably because she had caught me in the middle of great erotic fantasies about Yvonne and I had had to suppress them entirely in order to adjust to the change in my afternoon plans.

"Don't you ever open your shades?" she said. "It's like a hole in the ground in here."

"Shall I open them?"

"Yes, yes, open them."

I did and squinted in the sudden light and then sat

back on the bed and looked closely at Susannah. In the sun she did not look so gray. Perhaps I had already cheered her up a little.

"You don't look particularly like a mother," I said. Her motherhood was indeed something I could hardly accept without seeing the evidence of it in her arms.

"I am one just the same," she said.

"Where is he now?"

"Jeff's mother's looking after him."

"I wish I could see him," I said.

"Xavy, is it awful of me to run out on them all?"

"It's only for a weekend, isn't it? Jeff can cope."

But she did not want to talk about Jeff yet, so we left that subject, and our conversation meandered about and did little more to acquaint me with their current situation. We talked about what had become of the people they used to know around here, how her own family was, that Beth Twombley was engaged, that my therapy was still going well, and about the girls I had been involved with pseudo-romantically since she and Jeff had moved away.

When we had finished our tea, Susannah said, "Xavy, couldn't we go somewhere else and talk? It's stuffy here, and it's such a lovely fall day. We could walk over to Fresh Pond."

I was agreeable, though I would rather have stayed indoors. I said I would have to leave a note for someone who might be dropping by, and Susannah leaned over my shoulder as I wrote it. "Yvonne, eh? You didn't mention her," she said and tickled my stomach.

I helped her with her coat, then put on my jacket, stuck the note on the nail on my door, and we stepped outside. It was cold, despite the warm sun on our faces. Susannah's hair blew about in the breeze, and now it looked as red as it always had.

"Let's not go by the old place, let's go this way," she said, so we crossed the street and turned left along the railroad tracks. "I don't want to see it again. Have you been back there?"

"Just walking by."

"We got such a funny note from the Nilakanthas saying how clean we left it. Do you really feel like walking all the way to Fresh Pond?"

"I've plenty of time," I said. "Nothing to do but see you."

We took the underpass at Sacramento Street and soon were in a pleasanter neighborhood, shuffling through leaves on the brick sidewalk.

"You haven't told me much about Philip yet," I said.

"Philip's fine. He's a beautiful baby, very easy and relaxed. Doesn't look like either of us."

"I wish I could see him."

"I suppose I might as well ask you now, Xavy," Susannah said, putting her arm through mine as we walked along. "Jeff didn't want me to mention it to you, he wanted to write you about it later himself, but I think I ought to warn you. We're going to be having a christening in the spring, and we want you to be the god-father."

"What! You're going in for a christening?"

"So it seems. Would you mind?"

"No, of course not, I'm honored. What do I have to do besides make false promises in a church?"

"Oh, it won't be that bad. It's mainly a way to get you to come out and visit us. That's what matters to me anyway." She held my arm tighter.

"What's got into Jeff?" I said. "I suppose he'll want to rewrite the service, stick in a little Shakespeare. Will they accept a fallen-away Catholic as an Episcopal godfather?"

"I'm sure it doesn't matter. Zada's going to be the godmother."

"What's got into Jeff, I really wonder."

"You can argue it out with him when he writes you. I just thought I should prepare you. I don't want to think anymore about it now." And she let go of my arm.

It took us forty-five minutes to get to the pond, and we found the park crowded with people and dogs. Susannah suggested we walk around the pond to get away from everyone. It is a large reservoir closed off by wire fencing. There is a paved track around it where high school track teams practice, and then some small woods and beyond them a loud highway with neon signs sticking up above the trees. Halfway around the pond, we climbed a little ridge and sat in the leaves under a birch tree and looked out through the bare trunks at the water. There were ducks on it, and now and then their quacks blew our way. Susannah leaned back against me, and I put my arm around her from behind and rested my chin in her hair, friendly fashion.

"We haven't found any friend as good as you in Chicago, you know, Xavy," she said.

I squeezed her a little and let her go on talking, hoping she felt like it at last.

"There's no one who stops over and hangs around at odd times. There's no one we do things with. It'd just be nice to have you to go for walks with us in the park with the baby. You know? Jeff misses you very much too. He's become so solitary. We both have."

She tilted her head up to me, and I kissed her on the forehead. Then she looked back down at the leaves. She was picking at the ground with her left hand, getting her fingers dirty.

"I didn't tell you Mrs. Kimberk is going back to Dr. Olafsson once a month."

"No, you didn't."

"Well, she is. I'm not sure why. I wouldn't say Jeff has been much help to her. She worries about him so. She's a terribly reserved woman, don't you think? I didn't think so at first, she's so friendly, but she's terribly reserved when it comes down to it. I don't understand her."

A huge yellow leaf-sweeping machine rounded a bend on the paved track and made enough noise to keep us from talking. We watched it pass and waved to the orange-jacketed driver, who must have thought he was interrupting something. He gave us a thumbs-up sign as if to say, "Get on with it, kids!"

Susannah turned halfway toward me with one arm around my waist and her head on my chest looking at me. I had been having a few thoughts of the outrageous and remote possibility of our ending up spending the night together and also of the difficulty of confessing it to Lichty if it should happen and even the difficulty of confessing the thoughts themselves, which had already occurred and therefore would have to be confessed no matter what. And I became annoyed at the prospect of having to discuss it all, session after session, to discover why I had relapsed or even thought of relapsing. Lichty would say, among other things, that it was my way of getting angry with him for not having solved all my problems for me.

Susannah was still looking up at me from my chest. I doubled my chin to look straight down at her and kissed her on the forehead a second time.

"Sweet old Xavy," she said.

I stopped leaning against the tree, which had become uncomfortable, and both of us lay back in the leaves on our sides, face to face, my arms around her. I pulled her close to me and kissed her again, and then she started to giggle. I let her go, and she lay back and put the back of her dirty left hand over her mouth trying to contain herself.

"Susannah, good heavens," I said.

164

"I suddenly started thinking about poop again," she said and launched into mild hysterics. "I haven't thought about it for nine months. Why should I start thinking about it now?" She was holding her stomach and shaking.

"Because the last time we two were alone, you started thinking about it," I said. "It must be a subconscious association — being alone with Xavier Fereira sets off the poop reaction."

That put Susannah into even greater tremblings. "Xavy, come here," she said and pulled my face down over hers, looked at me, and stopped laughing. With a sudden frown, she said, "Xavy, you don't know how depressed I've been."

"No, I don't, but you haven't told me anything."

"I haven't, I'm sorry. I *am* sorry. Let's go back."

I stood up and helped her to her feet, and we stumbled down the ridge to the track and walked back around the pond, my arm on her shoulders, and aside from an occasional giggle from her, we did not say anything more. Now the high school track team was jogging by us one by one as we walked along.

Back at the entrance to the park, we played with an exuberant trio of dogs, a golden retriever, a little black spaniel, and an Irish setter; threw sticks for them, chased them about, and in general warmed ourselves up and revived our spirits. When a fat little puppy appeared on the top of a hill and our wild companions charged off to introduce themselves, Susannah and I took the opportunity to withdraw from all the rough-housing.

As we walked back across town, Susannah suggested we walk over to Zada's dorm but then decided not to. Zada would want to hear about Jeff, and Susannah still did not want to talk about him. So we walked on into the Square instead and did the sorts of things we used to do together, browsing about the bookstores and record stores. Susannah spent a lot of money and worried that Jeff would not approve. She bought me an advance Christmas present, Gieseking playing Mozart sonatas; and then I bought her one, Mann's *The Transposed Heads* in paperback, all I could afford.

Finally, we collapsed into a booth in the Burger Cottage and had an early dinner. As we ate, I thought as cool-headedly as my baser thoughts would permit me about the dilemma which would shortly present itself, what to do with Susannah next, and because I did not know what she wanted to do, I allowed myself to be entranced again with certain unlikely possibilities. She was still by far the most attractive girl I had ever taken to bed, and for all my loyalty to Jeff, I could not quite put aside the half-wish to retrieve the experience from what now seemed the mythical past.

When we stepped out into the dark and cold, I found myself saying as offhandedly as I could, "Well, Susannah, shall we go back to my apartment or what?"

Only a few minutes before, paying the check, I had resolved not to make any ambiguous proposals to Su-

sannah but to see that she got back to Ida Lee's unmo-
lested. I do not know why I went back on myself so
soon, but I must not have been thinking seriously.

"Do you want to?" she said.

"I'm afraid there's no other place I can take you. I'm
broke as usual."

"I don't expect to be taken anywhere, you know
that."

"I know. Well, shall we go back then?"

"All right. I'm very tired though, Xavy. I should
only stay for a while. All this walking, and Ida Lee and
I were up late last night talking and I promised her I'd
be back early."

It was mostly to cover up my baser thoughts that I
said, "I hope you'll do a little talking with me too, Susannah."

"It's only fair that I do, isn't it?" she said. Her arm
was back in mine, and we were walking the old familiar
route from the Square to Somerville Avenue. But she
did not begin her talking yet. Instead, we talked about
Gieseking's Mozart for a while and then about *The
Transposed Heads*.

Yvonne had left a note on the nail on my door re-
placing the note I had left for her. It said, "I'll forgive
you this once. Y."

"I hope that girl can take care of herself," said Susannah. I opened the door for her and followed her
into my apartment. "Because she won't get any help

from you." She took off her coat and stared sharply at me as I put the packages on the kitchen table.

"Look here, Susannah," I said.

"Look here what?"

I shrugged my shoulders and was silent and started washing the teacups in the sink. Susannah switched on the ceiling light and pulled down the shades. When I turned around, she was sitting at the foot of the bed, leaning her head on her bare arm on the brass bedstead, and her red hair was spread out concealing her face from me.

"Can't I criticize you at all, Xavy?" she said, without looking up. "You've always taken the littlest criticisms so hard. You should learn to be more resilient."

"I should, should I?" I said with a frown. I was suddenly very angry with her.

"Come here, funny old friend," she said to make up, looking up at me with a hesitant smile.

I sat down beside her, still angry, and she undid some of the snarls in my hair with her long fingers with the stubby fingernails. Then she kissed my nose, and I decided I did not want to be played with like that. I stood up again and stood in front of her, looking down.

"What do you expect me to do, Susannah?"

She looked worried and then put her head back on her arm on the bedstead and looked at the floor. I stood looking at her and soon had convinced myself that she was waiting for me, so I leaned over and put my arms under her arms and pulled her further up on the bed

168

and lay down first beside her and then on top of her.

It happened as it had happened once before, but instead of lasting a long time, it was very quick. I had been exuberant our first time, but this time I could not be. I could not enjoy what I was doing or have any hopes for it. I had to do it and get it done, and that was all.

Susannah began crying even before it was over and when it was, she hugged me almost with fury and cried at the same time. I was sweaty and exhausted. My heart was pounding against her, and I stopped kissing her and put my head beside hers in her hair and then closed my eyes, dreading to open them.

We did not move at all for several minutes, and at first I almost slept, but then I began to think that for two years I had wanted just this, to be in bed a second time with Susannah, and I became aware of each part of her that I was touching again after so long and became excited again but kept my eyes closed and did not kiss her. Susannah was unresponsive, so I turned on my side and she got up and went into the bathroom not looking at me.

I sorted out our tangled clothes and put my underpants back on and leaned up against the bedstead, managing to keep myself from thinking about what I had just done.

In ten minutes, Susannah came out with a towel around her and my hairbrush in one hand. "I've been in there trying to think of what to say," she said.

"Are you upset?"

She came and sat next to me and began to brush her hair. "I'm partly relieved."

"I thought you'd be disappointed to find I'm still the same old Xavy."

"But I expected you to be."

I took the brush from her and brushed her hair myself for a while.

"Don't you feel relieved too?" she said. "Hasn't it been hanging over you too?"

"Yes, it has," I said.

She turned her head and looked at me, and I put the brush down.

"You look very upset," I said. She shook her head, but I was beginning to realize what an appalling thing I had done. "Why did you cry like that?" I put my hands on her shoulders and looked closely at her green eyes. The eyelids kept blinking. They were thin and veiny and still touched with tears at the edges.

"I don't know what to do, Xavy," she said. "I don't know how to talk to you about it. I'm sorry. I needed to come to see you. You've been so lovely to me today."

She leaned against me, and I held her to me for several minutes while she cried again.

"Maybe I'll go back now and be happier," she said. She sat up and picked up the brush and began brushing again, looking across the room vaguely at a map on the wall.

"I didn't know what to do," I said. "I certainly shouldn't have done this. What if Jeff found out?"

"Don't think about that, Xavy. He won't."

But I could no longer keep from thinking about what I had just done. I leaned back against the bedstead and noticed that my hands were shaking, so I tucked them under my arms. Suddenly I wished Susannah would leave. I did not think I could bear watching her sitting there tearfully beside me brushing her hair.

She did leave quite soon. She would sleep better in her old apartment, she said, and Ida Lee was expecting her. There was no point in talking now anyway, when we were both so tired and confused. I walked her slowly to the Square, and we said good-night with a public kiss by the turnstile in the subway station. Then I walked home wondering if the progress I thought I had made with Lichty was any progress at all.

I tossed about all night and could not sleep. I got out of bed several times, turned a light on, and paced around my little apartment in my longjohns, shivering and trying to clear my head, but each time I returned to bed, I was as restless as before. At last, I looked over and saw a fine line of morning light under the window-shade by my bed.

Susannah called at seven thirty to say she had decided to take an early plane home because she wanted to get back to Jeff and her baby. I told her we had to talk, and she said it was better that we did not. She would see me in the spring when I came for the christening.

Surely we knew each other well enough, she said, not to have to spend hours mulling over our behavior the night before.

For two or three days I did not leave my apartment. Then I decided to set myself the self-disciplinary project of writing this book, to sort myself out, and now I have written as much of it as I am going to.

8

BACK in January, after finishing
the preceding page, I stuck the whole manuscript in a
manila folder in a drawer with a few other abandoned
literary projects of mine. But now it seems I must add
to it because I have just promised a certain person I
will let her read it. We have decided to keep nothing
from each other. But although I will do nothing to alter
the effect of a single word in the first seven chapters, I
do feel compelled to account for the deepenings and
widenings of heart which have occurred since. For if
she who is to read this book had to stop at the end of
Chapter Seven, she might well wonder if I really am the
sort of person she ought to consider marrying someday.

I trust I can recapture the tone and pace of what
I wrote several months ago. I will try to be leisurely

about what I have to report, though a certain excited impatience (the impatience which I was just beginning to feel when I stopped writing in January and which has been intensifying since then) makes me want to sum it all up now in one enthusiastic paragraph and have done with it. But I will discipline myself.

As soon as I had put the book aside, I began to cast about seriously for a job, not as a puppy-keeper or a paperback-seller but, on Jeff's suggestion, as a teacher. It was Zada who pointed out that some school might have a vacancy at the end of its first semester, so in a spurt of energy I wrote twenty-five nearly identical letters to private high schools in the Boston area.

Zada seemed as pleased as I was when I got offers from three of them, and Jeff and Susannah could hardly believe it when I phoned them to tell them the news. They were still at Jeff's mother's and had not yet decided which way to go.

The offer I accepted was from the Lukes School, an odd little institution for gifted but disturbed children whose parents had enough money to send them there. I was interviewed on a Saturday by Mrs. Lukes herself. I had expected a large lump of a woman, a Dr. Olafsson perhaps, so I was surprised to see a twitchy little lady opening the tall door of her office on the first floor of the converted Victorian house that housed her school.

"Mr. Fereira?" she said. "Do come in. You wrote a lovely letter."

I shook her hand, smiled, and followed her into a tiny office.

"This used to be the butler's pantry," she said.

I sat down on the red kitchen chair which she offered me with a tap on the top rung of its ladder back, and she sank into something soft behind her desk, almost disappeared, then pulled herself up and propped herself on her elbows.

"Now I can't pay you very much," she said. "I have to explain that at once. I can't apologize for it again."

"I don't expect too much, Mrs. Lukes," I said.

"Let me call you Xavier, and you call me Helen. The kids do too. I'll warn you they'll probably think up some interesting nickname for you — Savior, Behavior, something that rhymes. Now tell me what you'd like to teach them."

"I assumed you had an opening in English," I said.

"I have an opening, Xavier. I have two in fact. I don't stop to wonder what the opening is in. I have an opening for a teacher, plain and simple. Teachers are individuals like anybody else. Whatever you do, it will differ sufficiently from what my other teachers do. No, you can teach the kids whatever you like. If you can keep their attention, you've accomplished the first thing. Our kids are very clever. They won't listen to something if it's presented limply. They may be hard on you at first, but you'll end up one hell of a good teacher, I guarantee it."

I found myself becoming more relaxed, despite Mrs.

Lukes's unpredictable manner. A similar interview in years past would have finished me.

She shook the jangly bracelets on her left wrist and looked me in the eyes. "You know, Xavier, I have quite a time getting people to teach here. Many find my theories threatening. Luckily, it's part of my theory to hire whoever is willing to take on the job. So you may consider yourself hired."

"Could you tell me more about the school?" I said.

"Cold feet?"

"Oh no, I accept, no question about it. I wouldn't teach anywhere else."

"That's what I hoped you'd say," said Mrs. Lukes.

I had not exaggerated. Mrs. Lukes, by her oddity, had decided me. It would be exciting to try something a little odd, I thought.

"We have thirty kids, Xavier, fourteen boys and sixteen girls. The youngest is twelve, the oldest seventeen. School opens at eleven in the morning — you know how adolescents like to sleep late. It closes at five in time for them to hang around the Square before going home to their parents. We don't expect homework. We have no rules worth mentioning. Do you see what I'm trying to do? You may wear whatever you please. Be assured *they* do."

"This is probably a silly question, Mrs. Lukes . . ."

"Helen, Helen, get in the habit."

"Helen," I said. "But is anything ever actually accomplished around here?"

"Make no mistake about it, Xavier," Mrs. Lukes said, "the kids love this school. It's the best part of their lives. They'll do anything for it. Elly Olson once got them to sit through a whole Bruckner symphony. They may have been, as they say, a little stoned for the occasion, but they sat through nevertheless, and loved it."

"Does Elly Olson teach here?"

"Indeed she does."

"If it's the same Elly Olson, she used to go out with my roommate in college." It had surprised me to hear the name again. I had forgotten about Jeff's old flames.

"Very likely," said Mrs. Lukes. "You'll feel right at home then. But you probably won't get along with all of us. Don't give it a second thought. It's good for the kids to see us squabble. You can start with the second semester, February second. We give a short skiing vacation at the end of January. There aren't any class periods as such, but you're bound to have a crowd around you the first day because you'll be new. That's really all you need know, except I should say I have a great deal of confidence in you. You have a nice face."

She stood up, shook her bracelets again, and stretched her other hand toward me to shake hands. "Good-bye," she said. "I'll draw up a contract sometime. How does three thousand for the second semester sound?"

I had not expected half that and told her so.

"Nonsense, you're worth more, but I just don't have it," she said, shaking the big floppy purse that sat on

177

her desk, as if to prove there could not be more than three thousand dollars in it.

I took a little stumble on the front steps as I was leaving the school, but I picked myself up and headed for Zada's dorm in high spirits to tell her the news.

Zada had projects of her own. She had done an admirable job on her three papers (two As and a B plus) and was in a much better frame of mind for her exams at the end of the month. But she had accomplished something even more important. I had happened to mention how pretty she looked one night when we met for a hamburg and a movie. She had blushed and said she had been losing a little weight, claiming it was the worry over exams, but I knew she was for once not all that worried. Then she confessed she had been making a real effort to watch what she ate, and somehow the whole thing had suddenly caught on for her.

"Not that you were ever really heavy," I said.

"I was pretty chunky though, Xavy," she said. "Still am."

"No, just cuddly," I said and gave her a squeeze. "And besides, people grow up and lose a lot of adolescent weight. Their metabolisms change." I was theorizing, but it sounded logical, and I promised myself that when I got my first paycheck I would take Zada shopping for a new dress as a reward for her self-discipline and to make up for that silly scarf I had given her the Christmas she gave me the beautiful Nehru shirt.

On Groundhog Day in the evening, we celebrated

both my twenty-fifth birthday and my first day of teaching (I had been a great success with the kids and only hoped I could keep it up). We phoned Jeff to wish him a happy birthday too, and found that his own plans had begun to take shape at last. When spring came, he and Susannah and the baby would head for the Porcupine Mountains in the secondhand Jeep station wagon which Mrs. Kimberk was giving Jeff for his twenty-fifth birthday. And just before they left, Philip would be christened, and I promised to come out for it.

I looked forward to the trip, but it did not seem as important to me as it might have in the past. My life was more my own by then and no longer revolved around Jeff and Susannah Kimberk. I was even paying a little more attention to my own family. The date for my sister Susie's wedding had been set for the end of February, and my parents insisted I come up the weekend before for dinner, so the whole family could be together once before the wedding. My mother, in a generous mood, suggested I bring a friend, so I brought Zada. I had told her so much about my family that she was quite curious to meet them.

We took the train from North Station, and my older brother Mike met us at the station in my hometown. It was a gray day, as it always seems to be whenever I go home. There was slush on the ground but no snow to speak of. Mike, a slick-haired real estate broker, made his usual snide remarks about my appearance. Actually, I had tried to be tidier than usual, in honor of

Zada's new dress, the one I had bought her with my first paycheck.

We slid into Mike's yellow Mustang, Zada in the middle, and waited a bit for the windshield to unfog. Then we drove along Bridge Street, past the empty old mills, and up the hill to my parents' house. Mike was making polite conversation with Zada in his salesman voice.

"Zada's Jeff's sister," I said. "You remember Jeff Kimberk, my old roommate."

"No, I don't," said Mike.

"I guess you were never there when he came up for dinner," I said, but if Mike had made an effort he would have remembered hearing about Jeff — my parents talked about him so much.

It was appalling how little Mike seemed like my brother. I cringed whenever he opened his mouth. When we were little, he used to do such things as have me lie on my back while he stood over me, one foot on each side of my head, and then he jumped up as though he were going to stomp both feet in my face, but he always split them apart at the last second and landed back on either side of my head.

We were in my old neighborhood now, passing one quasi-Colonial house after another. When we moved there in the mid-fifties, the development was the show-piece of the town, and I suppose it still is because there has been no new construction in the town since. My parents bought classy new furniture (we had been living

180

down the hill where everything was run-down) and filled the bookshelves with figurines and hand-tinted photographs of each of us. Whenever I go home, I must be reminded of the way I looked when I graduated from prep school. It is the way my parents would always like to think of me.

My mother rushed out the back door as we drove up under the carport. She had on a white apron, which flapped about in the wind and was much too long for her. She is the shortest of us all.

"Well, Xavier, didn't think we'd be seeing you again so soon. Don't tell me you've put on a tie! Who's this?"

"Mother, this is Zada Kimberk, Jeff's sister."

My mother beamed. She had always adored Jeff. "Well, how nice! Zada, did you say? How do you spell it?"

"Z, A, D, A," I said.

"Zada and Xavier, almost rhymes. So this is Jeff's sister! Well, come on in, everyone else is here. First time in years we've had us all together, Robin too, I mean. You should see him, Xavier, he looks so fine, not a scar, not a scrape. Wipe your feet."

She hurried us into the kitchen while Mike kicked the slush out from under the fenders behind his tires. Susie came rushing in from the dining room and gave me a surprisingly untraditional hug.

"What's got into you, hot stuff?" I said.

"I'm just glad to see my grumpy old brother. Any

181

objections? So aren't you going to introduce me to your girl, Xavier?"

"Zada, this is Susie."

"Jeff's sister," said my mother in a whisper.

"Hi, Zada. It's really nice to meet you."

"Doesn't she look like Jeff?" said my mother. Zada does not look a bit like Jeff.

"Oh, here's Robin," said Susie.

Robin stood at the dining room door, propping it open with one foot, and extended his hand to me. When I had last seen him, he was a high school kid.

"Hello, Xavier," he said in his new sturdy voice. "Good to see you again." He was tall and handsome in an ordinary way. Susie was terribly short beside him. In fact, he made our whole family look somewhat stunted.

I introduced Zada once again and then went through it all once more when Tony, Lucy, and Mike's pregnant wife Linda came in. Mike tramped in the back door, and my mother started screeching, "Get out of the kitchen, everybody out of the kitchen, go on in the living room and bother your father, I've got to cook for ten, Lucy, you stay here and help."

On my way out, Lucy, whose hair is as fuzzy as mine, whispered to me, "Hi, Xavier." It was her private hello after her public one.

My father had been in the living room all the time, not bothering to get up from his corner of the couch to come out to the kitchen and greet us. "Well, if it isn't the working man," he said and put down his paper.

I introduced Zada. Realizing she was Jeff's sister, my father turned politically polite and stood up to shake her hand.

"I've always admired your brother, Zada," he said. "Wish some of his sense'd rub off on number two son here."

Zada made one of her embarrassed chortles and sat down safely beside me on the beige love seat. Susie and Robin sat opposite us on the ochre love seat, and Mike and Linda joined my father on the couch. Tony did not sit down right away but slumped in the doorway for a time before finding his way to one of the armchairs by the fireplace.

Then the animals made their entrance: first, two slender, aloof cats, Inca and Maya (they were Az's replacements and belonged to Susie); then Lucy's cat Scrowly, a revoltingly fat fellow who moved painfully slowly; and finally we heard a demanding scratch on the front door and Tony jumped up to let in Wolfgang, his dog, a combination Collie-Alsatian, or Collation, as I cleverly put it once. Wolfgang was slushy and made the mistake of putting a friendly paw on Zada's lap when he said hello.

"Oh, your dress!" said Susie with a squeal, and she dragged Zada upstairs to wash out the paw mark. I suspected that Susie was anxious to get Zada alone and interrogate her about me.

"Speaking of pets, how are your birds?" I said to

Linda to be conversational. Mike and Linda did not care for four-footers, but they had a sunporch filled with songbirds and African violets. Linda had a voice like a foghorn and was very tedious.

Scrowly settled on my lap, and now that Zada was gone, my father returned unsociably to his paper. Mike started pitching questions to Robin about "Nam," even though Robin clearly did not want to talk about it. Tony tapped Wolfgang on the nose, and the two of them left the room. Tony had become quite sullen and vague since he had been at college. I wished he would move into an apartment with some friends. He was so sensitive to things at home. Lucy was better insulated. She had none of Tony's touchiness but lived her own little private life with everything else going on around her.

She came in from the kitchen now and said, "I see you've got Scrowly on your lap. He misses you."

"How do you know that?"

"He likes to sleep in your underwear drawer."

Lucy settled on the floor in front of the fire. Scrowly blinked at her once and closed his eyes again. Inca and Maya had stretched themselves on the mantelpiece above Lucy's head. Lucy and I strongly resemble pictures of our paternal grandfather in his fisherman days. His name was Xavier too, and he had quite a crop of curly hair. Tony and Mike are as dark as Lucy and me, but their hair is only wavy. Mike is, as I said, slick and even sinister looking, but Tony used to be rather fresh and sweet, the best-looking one in the family. Now he is droopy and moody and so seems less attractive. Susie is even darker than the rest of us, and she makes up her eyes darkly and does ugly things to her hair, sprays and teases and sets it, even in this casual era.

"So who's your girl friend?" Lucy said in an undertone.

"She's Jeff's sister. She's not exactly my girl friend."

"Oh yeah? She's nice."

"Yes, she really is. She's very shy."

"I've found the nicest people are shy," Lucy said. "I'm shy myself."

"And you're the nicest person I know," I said.

"Well, I'm probably one of them," said Lucy with a grin. "Hey, Xavier." I leaned over the arm of the love seat to hear what she had to say privately. "Mom's off on a spin."

"She is, is she?"

"Is she ever!"

"Well, just try to be helpful."

"What do you think I do all day? I didn't see anyone else out there helping."

"It's Susie's wedding that's got her going," I said.

"I hope that's all it is," said Lucy. "I'm having trouble coping."

My mother came in, and my father put down his paper. "Everything's under control, where is everybody?" she said.

"Wolfgang put his muddy paw on Xavier's girl

friend's dress, and Susie took her up to wash it off, and Tony took Wolfgang somewheres else," said Linda in her foghorn voice.

"Where's my cigarettes?" said my mother, settling into the armchair by the ochre love seat. Robin jumped up to offer her one of his. "How's that for service!" she said. "I didn't see you leaping to your feet, Xavier Fereira."

"I don't smoke, Mother," I said.

"What have I missed? Have you been telling your father about your new job?"

"I was just about to get to that," said my father.

"I'm pretty well paid," I said, which seemed a diplomatic way to start off.

"I'm so glad you're teaching now instead of working on that book," said my mother. "I wasn't going to discourage you, but I sure had my doubts."

"I'll say," said my father. "Every jerk who gets involved in the student mess thinks he can write a book about it. Have you been down to the book department at Kelly and Selman's? Who reads that junk?"

"I don't read it either, Dad," I said. "I wasn't writing a political book."

Zada and Susie came back downstairs with Wolfgang at their heels.

"I thought Tony took that beast somewhere," said my mother.

"I don't know where Tony went," said Susie.

"How's the spot, Zada? Isn't that terrible, on such a pretty new dress!"

"Oh, it came right out, Mother, don't make a thing of it," said Susie, nuzzling in beside Robin who gave her a proprietary squeeze.

"Xavier gave me this dress," said Zada. She had noticed I was known in full as Xavier up here.

"Xavier!" said my mother with a screech. "He couldn't have picked out such a pretty dress, as tasteful as that. What do you call it? Sort of peach?"

"Apricot, I think," said Zada, smiling at me.

"You're putting your life on the line with this one, let me tell you," my mother said. "It was sheer luck he didn't pick out something with purple polka dots. Get down, Wolfgang!" (Tony had held a naming contest when he got his dog. I had won with "Wolfgang," a name quite out of place in our family.)

"Wolfgang, come here," said Lucy. Scrowly opened his eyes, decided he did not like Lucy putting her arms around Wolfgang's neck, and made the tremendous effort of jumping off my lap to demand her attention for himself. He has been Lucy's for ten years now. She puts up with his lazy and spoiled nature with infinite patience.

"Lucy, why don't you sit up off the floor?" said my mother.

"That's Tony's chair."

"You don't see him there now, do you? It looks

187

sloppy to see you on the floor. Wolfgang will just climb up there if you don't."

"Let him," said Lucy. "It's his favorite place anyway. My favorite place is the floor."

"Lucy, get up off the floor," said my father in his most disciplinary voice. But at that moment, Tony slumped back in and took his seat, and the family circle, animals included, was complete.

When there are animals in a room and the people present are at a loss for intelligent things to say, they usually end up talking about the animals. This is often the case in my family, and I think my parents have encouraged all the pets simply to have something to talk to guests about. Surely neither my father nor my mother is fond of them for their own sakes. They refer to them as "the beasts."

I had a dog of my own when I was growing up. Her name was Victoria, an Irish setter, and when she died I was at prep school and could not come home to see her for the last time. Victoria was a nervous dog and afraid of the dark, and she slept with me until I went off to school. She was the only thing I missed at home, but that was enough to make me terribly homesick.

In contrast, Wolfgang is entirely too sure of himself. There is no place he does not feel he has a right to be, nothing he does not have a right to do. My mother has given him up as hopeless, much as she has his master Tony. "Those two!" she often says, with a contemptuous snort.

According to my father, the only time the animals served a purpose was when he first ran for alderman five years ago and they appeared in the family photograph on his campaign brochure. Jeff used to kid me about that photograph, me in my cloddish short-haired days. It was even worse than the prep school graduation picture. I do not know how Jeff got hold of a copy, unless my doting mother (doting on him, that is) sent him one for laughs.

My father looks more impressive in photographs than in the flesh. He is a small, stocky, swarthy person, but he manages to make his jaw look especially firm and his swarthiness pass for a Florida tan when he is photographed. My mother is also small and dark, but plump in the way little people are, a little fat stomach and a fat little bottom, all the more noticeable because the rest of her is so delicate. Her first name is Alma.

The evening I am describing might well have been another boring, animal-centered one, but it turned out not to be. Robin's presence helped, but it was Zada who made the great difference. Jeff had that effect on my parents too. My mother was convinced that Jeff could do anything he set his mind to. My father always asked him to take a look at the hi-fi, and even though Jeff was as unmechanical as I, he managed to make a few clever adjustments and my father thought he was a genius.

Zada did not have Jeff's competent manner or his appealing openness — she was quiet and blushed slightly whenever she was addressed. But my parents could only think of her as Jeff's sister. I imagine my mother was already wild with the hope that something romantic might be developing between her second son and this sister of Jeffrey Kimberk himself.

We did talk about the animals most of the time before dinner, but they were banished from the dining room in honor of the special occasion, and so the conversation was forced up to the human level.

My mother had prepared a sizable feast, a turkey with the Christmas trimmings, and had set the table with the best cloth and all the fancy china and silverware, but of course none of it was old, and, snob that I am, I felt a little embarrassed by it in front of Zada, not that she paid any attention to such things.

Zada sat on my father's left and I beside her. On the other side of me sat Susie, and Robin beside my mother. Across the table was Lucy at my father's end and Tony at my mother's, with Mike and Linda in between. I remember the arrangement precisely because the scene that followed has stuck in my mind in clear images — Zada blushing behind her wineglass; Robin politely passing everything, Susie's eyes on him the whole time; Mike and Linda ignoring each other; Tony shoveling the food down; Lucy carefully composing each bite on her fork: a sliver of turkey, a few peas, a nibble of dressing, a dab of cranberry; and my father and mother, at either end, one stern, the other jittery; all by nondrip candlelight.

The men followed Robin's example and pushed in the chairs of the ladies to their left before they sat down. Then my mother made Tony get up and pour the Portuguese rosé. We seldom had wine with dinner. "And twist the bottle each time so it doesn't drip, and ladies first, all the way around. Be cooperative, Tony." Tony did his best to do it wrong.

"Don't fill it to the top," said Mike. "Give it room to breathe. Don't you know anything about wine?"

"Screw you," said Tony.

My father slammed his fist on the table, and Zada jumped. "Cut out the language, Tony Fereira. Sorry I startled you, Zada. This one doesn't hear unless he's yelled at."

"Let's not get on Tony," said Susie, "he's doing his best."

"That's not saying much," said Mike. Linda hushed him.

"Oh please!" said Susie. "This is going to be *my* wedding, isn't it, and I can't stand it if everybody's arguing. That's the only thing I ask for, for everybody not to argue, just for one week, please!"

"Do you remember at Jeff's wedding?" I said to Zada. "There was something about me picking up a ham. I'm sure he never really explained it to me. And then there we were back at the reception and I hadn't got the ham."

"Typical," said my mother. "I couldn't count on you for an I-don't-know-what. I've learned my lesson with

191

this one long since, Zada. I'm not counting on him for a thing next week, not a thing. If he shows up on time, it'll be more than a miracle. Let alone pick up a ham. Not on your life!"

"Oh, Mother!" I said. I hoped Zada was aware that my mother was laying it on thick for the effect. It was her peculiar way of making her son sound appealing to a girl, as if she were saying, "I'm glad you're taking this fellow off my hands at last." But I do not think Zada understood that kind of humor.

"But really, Mrs. Fereira," she said, "Jeff was pretty awful at his wedding. I'm sure the ham was entirely his fault. He got very impossible."

"I won't believe a word against Jeff," said my mother. "He's my favorite favorite. Mike, you didn't ever meet him. I know Tony did. Lucy had a crush on him."

"I did not," said Lucy.

"You all ought to be like Jeff, you boys. Of course, Robin here does pretty good . . ."

"Just wait till you're an official family member, you'll get it too," said Susie, giving my mother a black frown with her eyebrows.

"But as for the rest of you!" my mother said, with a "Dear Lord, save us" expression. "Oh, I'm only kidding, you're all unimpeccable."

"What's that supposed to mean?" I said.

"That's the word, isn't it?"

"No, Mother," said Lucy.

"I think it's time the working man told us about his

new profession," said my father with a challenging look in my direction. I had been afraid he would renew the subject.

"Yeah, let's hear about it," said Mike in his transparently uninterested way. And everyone perked up his ears, even Tony.

"You'd probably all think the school was crazy," I said. "It's a little school, the Lukes School, for smart rich kids with disturbed minds."

"Lord God!" said my mother. "They don't call it that?"

"No, no, but that's what it is. Mrs. Lukes is an original character, to say the least."

"Who's Mrs. Loots?" said Tony.

"She runs the place. Let him tell it. Pay attention," said my mother.

"You'd get a kick out of her, Tony," I said. "The kids can wear whatever they like, there are no rules, school doesn't even begin till eleven, no homework, no class periods."

"Fuckin' A!" said Tony under his breath, but my parents did not hear or else they chose to ignore him.

"What grade do you teach, Xavier?" said foghorn Linda.

"No grades either. I just teach whatever bunch of kids gathers around me."

"This school can't be accredited," said my father.

"I think it is," I said. "Mrs. Lukes is a respected educator."

"I'll bet," said my father.

"She is."

"That's what I said. I don't doubt it."

"Well, anyway, that's the school. I get along with most of the other teachers. There are some oddballs."

"No kidding!" said my father. He sat back in his chair and made a scornful little laugh. His sarcasm was not quite as well-meant as my mother's.

"Any nymphos in the bunch?" said Mike.

"Mike!" said Linda.

"I can't really say, Mike," I said, taking him utterly seriously. "There's a rather liberated girl named Elly Olson, but I wouldn't call her a nympho."

Zada looked at me with a startled expression which I caught out of the corner of my eye. I had not mentioned Elly to her before.

"Doesn't sound like a job to me," said my father. He sat forward and looked me in the eye, firming up his jaw.

"That's what I like about it," I said. "It's like not having a job."

"Sometime you might think about having a real job," my father said.

"What's the difference if I'm getting paid? Look, I'll be getting six thousand for eight months' work. Can't beat that."

"With your degree?"

"So what?" I said.

"Look, I don't care what kind of salary you get,"

said my father. "But you've got more talent in you than just teaching in some quack school." Of course, he was perfectly right.

"I'm going to get dessert ready," said my mother. "Come on, Lucy, and help."

"I was hoping for once this was more of a serious job, Xavier," said my father.

"Who says it's not serious?"

"Come on, what kind of charlatan is this dame?"

"Mrs. Lukes? She's brilliant!"

At the other end of the table, Tony got up with a disgusted look.

"Sit down, Tony, no one excused you."

"I have to go check on Wolfgang."

My father slammed his fist on the table again and said, "That dog can take care of himself!"

Zada jumped, and I could see she was upset, though I had already forgotten my mention of Elly Olson and now attributed her upset entirely to my father's behavior.

There was silence while Tony sat down and then more silence. I took a sip of wine and tried to appear calm. Then I heard Zada begin speaking in a hesitant way but with the smallest edge of righteous anger in her voice. Her hands were shaking, so she put them in her lap.

"But Mr. Fereira," she said, "don't you think it's good Xavy's doing this? I mean not just for the kids' sake. I'm sure they're very disturbed and need help, and I'm sure regular school doesn't work for them. But it's also good Xavy's doing this for his own sake. He was really stuck before. I don't mean he'll be doing it for the rest of his life. But when I think of my brother and how messed up he's been lately . . ."

"Jeff messed up?" said my father.

"Jeff's sort of stuck now. He doesn't know what he wants to do, and he's given up on his social work, and he's going off to the woods. It's completely absurd. I'm really worried about him. He's so theoretical about it. You can't talk practically with him anymore."

My mother had caught the end of Zada's little speech, having crept back in when her curiosity got the better of her. "I can't believe Jeff doesn't know what he's going to do," she said. "He's always doing interesting things. He's just going through a phase. Lots of people do, Zada. It's the ones in the perpetual phase, like some of these monkeys here, you have to look out for."

My father could see that Zada was being very serious, so he said no more.

"I'm going to check on Wolfgang anyway," said Tony, picking an advantageous moment.

"Strawberry shortcake, Tony," my mother called after him.

"I don't want any," said an already distant voice.

Susie got up to help clear the table and, with a nervous gesture, tipped her wine glass into the sweet potatoes and broke into tears.

"I knew nobody paid attention when I asked you not to argue," she said with a sad whimper.

Mike threw her his napkin to wipe up the wine, but the dish had caught it all.

"Oh, God dammit," said Susie, spluttering tears. Mike was laughing, but I kept my amusement to myself. Robin put his arms around Susie and held her close to him, and he looked past her as he patted her back and smiled a comradely smile at me. Perhaps he figured the best way to handle the Fereiras was to keep quiet.

I hope I have not portrayed my family as a pack of fools. I cannot be fair to them, at least not at this stage of my life, so let me put them aside again, now that I have given some idea, warped perhaps, of what I have waiting for me at home, and let me treat with more seriousness the conversation between Zada and me as we sat side by side in the almost empty train coming back to Boston.

Zada had taken her furry winter coat off because the car was overheated and piled it on the pair of seats facing us, along with an old red and green striped scarf of Tony's which my mother had insisted I take back with me for warmth.

"I don't suppose I should've talked like that at dinner, Xavier," Zada said. "I like calling you Xavier. You never told me you were called Xavier at home. I hope I didn't alienate your father by saying all those things."

"It did him good, I was proud of you," I said. "Actually it was a mild evening for them. Sometimes we do nothing but scream at each other. Oh, I forgot to tell you. You know what Tony said to me as we were leaving? 'Hey, Xavier, I dig your chick.' "

Zada turned quite red. "I felt sorry for Tony," she said. "He seemed so detached."

"I think he's been taking drugs," I said.

"Oh, poor thing," said Zada, with a downcurling of her lower lip.

Zada is a girl who takes people to heart. It is not a sentimental trait. I do not know how she has managed it, having been shy and a wallflower most of her life, but she reacts to people in a direct way. Take Susannah for contrast. With Susannah I was constantly aware of Susannah herself. A meal cooked by Susannah was, without question, Susannah's particular meal. Her piano playing was particularly Susannah's, as it should have been if she aspired to be an artist, but that is not quite what I mean. Her Schubert, for instance, was Schubert channeled through Susannah, not Susannah channeled through Schubert. In other words, she put her subjective stamp on things, and that was not always good. When I was with Susannah, she put her stamp on *me*. It was Susannah's day, Susannah's walk to Fresh Pond, Susannah's browsing in stores and supper at the Burger Cottage. If Susannah's mood was jolly, then the day was jolly too.

Perhaps I am being unfair to her, but it is true that

she had a tendency to try to attract, to sit serene and beautiful, or sometimes troubled and beautiful, and to draw others to her. I suspect that could become rather tedious in a marriage. The difficulties she and Jeff are having may not all stem from Jeff's behavior. He is off the track, unsure and confused, but he may also be a little disappointed in his wife. She has become all inward-going and without resources, either in herself or in other people. It is clear from her behavior with me last November. She did not come to share in my friendship, whatever she may have said, but to appear before me and have the desired effect. I am convinced of that now, but at the time, of course, I blamed myself for everything that happened.

Zada has never made me feel bad about myself. I always feel *better* when I have been with her. But the night coming back on the train, I had only the first inkling of what makes her a superior person. All I sensed then, most of it subconsciously, was that this girl, young and uncertain as she was, had the adult ability to be objective about people and to take them truly to heart. I sensed this in her round friendly eyes looking directly at me (no blank stares such as Susannah might resort to, an attention-getting device, passive-aggressive behavior, says Lichty) ; in the way she wore her new apricot dress more for what it was (my present to her) than for what she made it; and in her bare legs awkwardly crossed, not as horsy as they had been two years ago, in fact considerably slimmer, but still clearly the legs of Zada Kimberk, the person, not the disembodied angel's legs of her sister-in-law.

"Tony's very handsome," said Zada after we had both silently reflected for a time on what I had said about Tony taking drugs.

"Yes, he's the best-looking Fereira," I said.

"I prefer you though," said Zada. She looked at me more bashfully than she ever had. "I love your face, Xavier. You have a very mild face. You have a mild nature too." I had the feeling she was making herself say these things at last after having wanted to for some time.

"And you like that?" I said.

"Oh yes, it's the pleasantest kind of person to be with. Who wants to be rushing around having traumas all the time?"

"I suppose I'm mild at heart, if I could get over a few things and settle down."

Somehow my old fears that I might be encouraging Zada in a hopeless romance were not aroused at this point. Perhaps I no longer feared it. We watched the dark warehouses, factory yards, and dumps go by. Lights on tall poles threw interesting shadows here and there. Most of the snow had melted.

"Who's this Elly?" said Zada all at once.

I felt a sudden pain in my chest and stomach. I realized how stupid I had been to mention Elly in that old-Xavy way at dinner. I put my arm quickly around

Zada's shoulders and pulled her head over to mine. "Elly's no one you have to worry about," I said.

I had never come out with a statement like that before, and I hardly knew I had said it. Zada looked up at me from my shoulder, startled. "Worry?" she said.

"I'd rather be with you," I said.

We said nothing the rest of the trip. Neither of us could take it any further. We each seemed to the other to be asleep, resting peacefully together. In North Station we changed to the subway, and we got laughing about the evening we had just spent. It seems Zada thought Linda was hysterically funny, and she did a good imitation of her foghorn voice.

I said good-night to her on the steps of her dorm. I knew that beneath her matter-of-fact thanks for the nice evening was a cautious ecstasy, and I detected a bit of it in myself as I walked home alone, with Tony's old scarf blowing about me in the wind.

9

A FEW evenings later, Zada startled me with a belated piece of news during a long soul-searching we were having in a corner of the crowded Burger Cottage — it seems she had lost her virginity in the midst of exam week with a fellow named Ivan Seymour whom she had met in her Primate Behavior course. I had no idea she had had any sort of an affair and was terribly hurt she had not told me about it sooner. But after, the first hurt feelings subsided, I found myself strangely relieved. She suddenly seemed less fragile.

Zada told me her news in a steady voice but looked at her plate the whole time and not at me. She had not wanted to tell me, she said, but now she felt she had to. "Now?" I said, but she kept looking at her plate, pok-

202

ing a last French fry in a blob of ketchup, and said no more. We were not yet able to discuss how our private thoughts about each other had developed recently.

I took it for granted from the start that this Ivan was not going to threaten my standing with Zada, for she did not express any excitement about him, did not even describe him. I have since modified this smug presumption of mine to take into account the complexities of Zada's feelings. She was still unsure of me and understandably had allowed herself the pleasure of becoming a little infatuated with Ivan.

I met him the very next morning when Zada and I were having a makeshift breakfast before her class. He had seen us crossing the street together and tracked us into the restaurant. Zada jumped slightly when she looked up and saw him, and I could not help feeling sour, though I doubt if my face showed it. Ivan was of radical appearance, tall and gangly with stringy brown hair over his shoulders. I was amazed to see that he had appropriated as a neckerchief the scarf I had once, given Zada, my silly first gift to her. She made a point of asking for it back as soon as Ivan sat down with us, and he with some grumbling undid the elaborate knot he had tied in it and passed it across the table to her. I suspected this Ivan made a career of picking out virginal classmates of the unthreatening variety and performing the desired service. I did not like to think of Zada as one of his prey.

I disliked him from the start, but during the twenty-

minute conversation that followed, I accumulated a
supply of rationalizations for my dislike. He took intellectual charge of the situation, or so he thought, but
his mind appeared to be interested only in the esoteric
and obscure. Who were my favorite composers? Schubert, Brahms? How dreary. I obviously had not discovered the quarter-tone music of Alois Hába. And now
that the Nielsen revival had run its course, the man to
watch for was Bax. Ivan Seymour himself would be
glad for a Havergal Brian boom, but none seemed im-
minent. Zada paid close attention to all this drivel. I
trusted she was merely being polite.

Ivan was apolitical and proud of it. Only sex and
art interested him, he said, with a nonchalant glance at
Zada. If Jeff had been there he would have fallen sullen and ignored the creep or else told him what he
thought of him. "I think you're a prize jerk," he might
have said. Jeff was able to say such things. But I acted
as polite as Zada, the two of us smiling at Ivan's clever-
nesses and intrigued to hear more about the esoteric
authors he admired so. No, I hadn't read Marcel La-
trine. I really should. Who? Heinz-Ulrich Badenzim-
mer? I was sorry I just hadn't kept up with things very
well. "I thought you said you were an English major,"
said Ivan. In the midst of my politeness, I had to remind myself that this character had taken Zada to bed.
It made me furious, so I tried not to think of it.

They went off to their class, and as I walked to work
I could not put out of my mind the image of the two of

them crossing the street together. I had always thought of Zada as entirely my own to squire about.

The kids drove me crazy all day. I was helping a bunch of them prepare a play for tape recorders. We had six recorders going, each one with the dialogue of a different character, and were trying to synchronize them so they could all talk to each other. It was a spectacular idea, I thought, but hard to execute. Kids from Elly's bunch were painting an antipollution mural in the hall and kept charging into the room and spoiling our timing. Finally, I grumbled something about Elly having gone too far with her laissez-faire attitude and stomped into the hall to find her. "Tell her to go screw," said fat little Betsy Rafferty, the authoress of the recorder play, who was the only one besides myself taking it as seriously as it deserved.

I was glad to be home that evening. I had bought a meatball sub at the sub shop down the street, and now it sat before me on its ketchup-soaked wax paper wrapping as I lay on my bed, somewhat at my wit's end from thinking about Zada and that Ivan all day. As I ate the sub, I worked myself up for what I knew would be an important phone call.

After a few preliminary pleasantries I said, "That character was really revolting, Zada, I'm sorry to have to say so."

"He's sort of affected, I guess," she said.

"He's not just affected, I think he's somewhat sinister. That's not the kind of first experience you should have had. People like that aren't worth it. They're all a put on." I had no business lecturing her like that, but I felt like being unreasonable for a change.

"Well, dammit, Xavy!" Zada said, suddenly annoyed with me and a little shaky-sounding. "It's a good thing it happened. Maybe it wasn't the best way for it to happen, but at least it did, and I actually like Ivan a lot, even if you think he's hard to take. He gets defensive in public. How would you expect him to act seeing me with an older, more sophisticated guy?"

"Nobody has to act as esoteric as that."

"Dammit, Xavy, I'm glad I didn't tell you about it sooner. You'd have spoiled it for sure. Look how much good it's done as far as I'm concerned. He changed the whole way I think about myself."

"But things were going better for you before you even met him. He just happened to appear at the right time."

"I don't care. Maybe it just happened to be him, but it was him nevertheless."

I was furious that she did not think I had had anything to do with it, after all the hours I had spent helping her out. "But it shouldn't have happened that way," I said. "You can't possibly have fallen for that fool."

"What do you know about it, Xavy? It may have been really nice, or won't you give me credit for that? Just because you have your Ellies and Yvonnes or whatever their names are. How do you know? Do you think I'm just a stupe?"

She hung up the phone with a slam, and I imagine she ran back to her room and cried.

Then I knew what I had to do. It was wrong to disapprove of Ivan if I was not going to show her how he could be improved upon. I was all of a sudden aware of my inclination to do so.

I went to her dorm, called her floor, apologized, and asked her to put on her coat and come out with me. She was downstairs almost immediately, still wiping her eyes but smiling expectantly with each sniffle.

I start a new section here because I cannot continue the description of that evening. I know that I faithfully recounted my two seductions of Susannah. But now this is a different matter, a matter only for Zada and me. And even if Zada is the only person who reads this book (as she will be — it could not possibly be read by anyone else, except of course Lichty), the first time we slept together is still not to be told. It must not be fixed in words. I might leave something out that was of extreme importance to her. I could not make it the way it was to her any more than I could make it the way it was to me. I have remembered it a hundred times differently. I would have to write it a hundred times, and then keep writing it, and it would still be diminished.

So let there be a little blank space in the story here, and then let me begin again with the long-delayed dénouement. I am sitting here on my brass bed, the sheets crinkled in the sunlight (Zada is at class), a free afternoon of writing ahead of me. Mrs. Lukes declared a holiday today so everyone could enjoy the beautiful weather.

Zada and I took the evening plane to Chicago for Philip's christening. I got by on youth fare, pretending to be my brother Tony. Zada and I were still quite cautious about our involvement with each other and reluctant to take it for more than it yet was. Dr. Lichty was delighted with me. I have not had much occasion to mention him lately. He is fading out of my considerations, or perhaps he has sunk so deep in them that I no longer need to think of him. He has begun to talk about terminating, but he too is not anxious to do anything rash. There is time, all things take time, and I agree with him. But I am actually in love with Zada Kimberk. I have never felt the feeling before, so I know how uncommon and rare it is. And I do not feel the need to analyze it with Dr. Lichty anymore because I am certain of it.

Jeff and Susannah and the baby met us at the airport. As we walked into the waiting room, there they stood on the other side of the railing which we had to walk around to get to them. Susannah held Philip with his head on her shoulder. Jeff had his arm around Susannah's waist. They were a little family already, standing there with delighted smiles. They did not move till we got around to them. I thought they looked too young to be parents, but in another moment they seemed older and a little tired.

Zada ran up to them ahead of me, anxious to see how Philip had grown. Susannah put her free arm around Zada and held the baby up with the other. Jeff patted his sister on the back and then stuck out his hand to me and pulled me toward him and patted me on the back too. I gave Susannah a kiss and then took a close look at the newest Kimberk. He was bigger than I had expected, quite a lump in fact, with dark brown hair and big eyes. He waved his hands about and looked me in the eyes, breaking into a satisfied smile. I could not see much of either Jeff or Susannah in him. He looked more like Zada than anyone else.

"Philip, this is your Uncle Xavy," said Jeff. Zada and I exchanged a private look.

"What do you think, Xavy?" said Susannah.

"It's hard to believe."

"Why should it be hard to believe?" Jeff said. We had already started walking down the corridor.

"I was wondering if you'd bring Philip," said Zada.

"Philip goes everywhere," said Susannah.

"It's almost spring weather at last," Jeff said. "We're hoping to get off next week."

"You're really going up to Michigan, Kimberk?"

"To the Porkies. We're really going. Shit, Xavy, I haven't seen you for over a year!" He grabbed my hair and shook my head with it.

"Ouch," I said.

Zada looked around at us happily and then back at the baby. We were all in good spirits. Only Susannah seemed a little subdued and dreamy. She had one of her familiar Indian mini-dresses on. It occurred to me she probably had not had a new dress in a long time.

We waited for our luggage — I took Zada's and Jeff took mine. "There's the Grizzly," said Jeff pointing out his Jeep in the floodlit parking lot.

"Jeff has a penchant for giving names to things," said Susannah.

"They call this color Turd Brown."

"Please, Jeff," said Susannah, actually irritated with him. I caught her eyes in a frown, so she forced a little laugh in my direction and sat in front with Philip. Zada and I climbed in back.

Jeff was in an especially good mood and entertained us all the way home with tales of the marvelous things they planned to do in the North Woods, step-by-step directions for building a log cabin, what to look for in mushrooms and wild berries, warnings of bears and even wolves.

Zada asked if she could hold Philip, and Susannah said, "Gladly." I found him fascinating to watch. It had been a long time since Lucy was a baby, and I had forgotten how inquisitively grabby they are and what fat knees they have. Philip kept looking at me with a puzzled expression but finally broke into another smile, punctuated by a glistening drool.

Mrs. Kimberk came running down the back steps as we pulled to a stop in the driveway. Zada gave me Philip to hold and jumped out and ran to give her mother a hug. I knew what kind of reunion it was for mother and daughter. Zada had written her mother when she had first been involved with Ivan Seymour, so Mrs. Kimberk knew Zada was no longer her virgin child. But she did not know about me.

I held Philip as gently as I could and stepped out.

"Well, Xavy!" said Mrs. Kimberk, still holding Zada, the two of them standing in the light from the open back door. "You've already been hired as baby-sitter, I see. Here, let me give you a kiss. It's been such a long time. We're so glad you could come for this. Zada, you look awfully thin." Mrs. Kimberk looked into Zada's eyes with sudden concern.

"Wait till you see Zada's new shape," I said.

Zada unbuttoned her trench coat and said, "See, I've lost a little weight."

"Good Lord, Zada, you have," said Susannah.

Jeff was startled. Zada did look so much better. She had on another new dress which I had bought her. It was more flattering than the apricot one, plum colored and rather short and a bit tighter than Zada was accustomed to. As we walked up the back steps, Mrs. Kimberk turned and whispered to me with a twinkling eye, "It's been a successful semester for her, Xavy!"

"Yes, it has," I said and patted Philip's bottom which seemed a little moist to me.

It was already late in the evening. Mrs. Kimberk went right up to bed, and Zada, Susannah, and the baby soon followed. They all knew Jeff and I had not seen each other in over a year and wanted to give us a chance to talk alone.

At that point, I knew Jeff was still my closest friend. When he left Boston, I had assumed we would drift apart for good, but I had had little experience with long-term friendships and was not yet aware that in the best of them you do not drift apart, that they can be picked up again with no loss of intimacy after months and years of separation. I had always thought you had to be with people constantly to count them as friends, but that was a paranoid point of view. Now Jeff and I started talking as familiarly as we had in the past, and I was sure I would always have him that way.

Scene: The Kimberks' front parlor with pale blue armchairs facing each other on either side of the fireplace, Xavy in one, Jeff in the other, both coincidentally dressed alike in blue jeans, workshirts, and sandals; one squat copper table lamp lighted, the Schubert A-minor quartet drifting in from the speakers in the back parlor.

Jeff: Do you think I'm crazy, Xavy?

Xavy: I've always thought so.

Jeff: I'm serious.

Xavy: What, for going to the woods?

Jeff: That, and everything else I've been doing.

Xavy: You're no crazier than anyone else.

Jeff: I'm certainly crazier than you.

Xavy: You're just making up for the days when I was the crazier one.

Jeff: You were never really crazy, Xavy. You were depressed and feeling victimized. But you weren't wild, you didn't make radical changes. Someone who's always making radical changes must be a little crazy.

Xavy: As long as you're aware of your problem, there's hope for you, Kimberk.

(*Xavy is being too light-hearted. Jeff, who had been so jolly earlier in the evening, now wants to be serious. He takes a whiff of his adrenalin inhaler which he now uses regularly to ward off the wheezes.*)

Jeff: What do you think about Susannah?

Xavy: I don't know, she still seems a little low.

Jeff: She's been like that for months. It's not good for a baby to have such a depressed mother. And my own mother's depressed too, you probably couldn't tell. And here I am in a manic state myself.

Xavy: Jeff, you're perfectly sane.

Jeff: I know. Sane and doomed.

Xavy: Come on, Jeff, you'll be off in the woods in a week and things'll perk up. It's hard living with your mother when you've got a new baby.

Jeff: Shit, it's easier. She takes care of him half the time. (*Pause.*) Did Susannah talk about everything when she was in Boston?

Xavy: No, that was the problem. She wouldn't talk about anything. I didn't know quite what to do.

Jeff: You must've done something for her. She was

better when she came back, but then she got feeling low again.

Xavy: Jeff, don't you think she just has to get out of here? (*Jeff shrugs his shoulders and gets up to turn over the record. He returns with two glasses of port.*)

Jeff: Xavy, have you noticed that all I can do is talk about myself? I'm absolutely obsessed with my own condition. I've been driving Susannah crazy.

Xavy: Don't blame yourself for everything. That's what I used to do.

Jeff: It's going to be difficult making the move. I'm in such a rut here. I don't give Susannah enough, Xavy.

Xavy: Oh, come on, Jeff, stop being so hard on yourself.

Jeff: I'm being revoltingly dreary, aren't I?

Xavy: Look, I want to talk about it, if you'll talk seriously, but it's no good just to whine and moan. (*Pause while they sip their port.*) I think things'll work out once you get out of here. And eventually you should all come and live in New England again, that's what I think.

Jeff: Maybe so.

Xavy: When you've got the hang of the woods.

Jeff: Maybe so. (*Pause.*) Let's talk about you instead. Who're you chasing after this month?

Xavy: (*Tempted to say, but thinks better of it.*) Do you really want to know?

Jeff: What I really want to know is if you're happier than you were.

Xavy: Much happier.

Jeff: You seem so. I can't believe it. How's it with Lichty?

Xavy: Drawing to a close.

Jeff: Really? Did you know my mother's back in therapy? (*Xavy nods.*) Surrounded by gloom and doom. It's up to you, Fereira, to put some jollity back in this place.

Xavy: Philip seems plenty jolly.

Jeff: Oh yes, he's jolly. He's our saving grace. When I think of him, I'm ashamed of myself for feeling low. (*Long pause.*) Xavy, we've missed your company more than anything else this past year. Maybe that's why everything's falling apart. You used to make such a difference in our lives, put things in a certain perspective. It's been very lost without you. Hey, what about this crazy school you're teaching at?

The conversation continued through the rest of the quartet and the second Schubert trio. I had much to amuse Jeff with. The Lukes School (and Elly Olson, out of the past) had to be described in detail, and so did my sister's grandiose wedding. When I told about how Tony was seriously busted a few weeks ago, it brought us back to our encounter with the state police in the days when Susannah was deciding whether or not to marry Jeff, and I was reminded secretly, as I am now and then, of the way I used to feel about the two of them.

We went up to bed quite late and had a few last words on the balcony at the head of the stairs.

"Isn't Zada in good shape!" said Jeff. "It really pleases me."

"Me too."

"Xavy, there's something I should tell you in case you don't know already. Maybe I shouldn't tell you, but I will anyway. Zada finally succeeded with boys. I think that's why she's blossoming out so. Did you know about it?"

I nodded.

"She probably doesn't think I know. Don't tell her. But she wrote Mother about it when it happened, and you know Mother couldn't keep it to herself, it worried her so. What do you know about it?"

"It was a good thing."

"It's so strange, Xavy, to think of my little sister . . ."

I nodded again and smiled.

"Sleep well," he said.

"Okay, Jeff, see you in the morning."

"I'm glad you're here, Fereira."

"So am I."

I was once more ensconced in the guest room with the cartoon books, and once more I found myself leafing through them before I could fall asleep. Zada was probably sound asleep on the other side of the wall.

I came down for breakfast late by the standards of a household regulated by a baby. Zada had taken Philip for a walk in his buggy, and Jeff and Susannah were in the village stocking the so-called Grizzly with various canned provisions, so I was alone with Mrs. Kimberk in the kitchen. She seemed much the same to me. She still wore odd combinations of clothes, cashmere and khaki, was still plump and short of breath, and I felt as comfortable with her as I always had.

She scrambled my eggs while I saw to the toast. Then she sat down across from me with her coffee but declined a piece of toast for herself, saying she had already eaten too much. I told her how much I had been looking forward to her cooking.

"As usual, you could use a little fattening up, Xavy," she said.

Then we talked about Zada and her thinning down, but it soon came out that Mrs. Kimberk was even more interested in hearing about this Ivan Seymour. She sounded embarrassed when she mentioned his name, but her curiosity had got the better of her. I told her I had met Ivan and had not liked him.

"Oh, but that's natural. I'm sure Jeff won't like him either. But what's he like?"

"I just found him too pretentious in a college sort of way, I guess."

"Well, you have to remember, Xavy, you're a lot older than Zada. He's probably just the thing for her, very impressive."

217

"I don't know. I think she's smart enough to see through him."

"Now Xavy, you mustn't be too critical and spoil him for her. It's her first such thing, you know. She's still seeing him, isn't she?"

"I suppose so. They're in a class together." I considered telling Mrs. Kimberk that Ivan was already in the past but decided that was for Zada to tell.

"Oh, Xavy, I'm sorry for prying like this. I really must stop. But do you know, Zada hasn't even brought a picture of him. She's as bad as Jeff was about Susannah, remember? Why don't I have more communicative children!" I put another slice in the toaster, and Mrs. Kimberk said, "Oh, put one in for me after all."

We were quiet for a while, and then she said, "You'll keep an eye on her, won't you? But don't let her get to be a bother. You've already done more than your share as a substitute older brother."

"Zada's never a bother," I said. "She's grown up lately, Mrs. Kimberk."

I was feeling as internally delighted as I have ever felt. The sweetness of the feeling was all the more so because it still had to stay inside and shape itself and then be even a little overripe before I could let it break forth. It would be a happy process.

That evening, Susannah and I cooked the dinner as a favor to Mrs. Kimberk, who needed a respite before the Twombleys arrived the next day. Jeff only got in the way in the kitchen, sticking his fingers in things, so we made him entertain the baby in the front parlor. Zada was out for the evening at her old friend Cathy's house.

Susannah and I had decided to prepare an elaborate version of the hamburg dish we had once made together two and a half years ago. She stood at the sink washing spinach piece by piece while I chopped mushrooms.

"I'll be glad when we're at last on the road," she said. "Hand me that colander, Xavy, thanks."

"Is there a paring knife?" I said. "This isn't sharp enough."

Susannah tugged at a sticky drawer, and the utensils inside shook into new positions when it shot open. I spotted what I needed.

"What was I saying?" said Susannah.

"About your going."

"Oh, I'm going to be so glad, Xavy."

"What are you doing for a piano in the woods?"

"Isn't it funny how I have to lug one of those things around with me wherever I go? We'll probably find an old one up there. We had to sell the one my parents gave me."

"How do they feel about the move?"

"My parents? Oh, they're skeptical. They seem to have lost their faith in Jeff, and he knows it. It worries him a lot. Hasn't he told you how he's dreading their coming tomorrow?"

"I'd have thought your father would admire you both for setting off like this."

"Are you kidding? When he heard about the trust

fund, he practically fell off his chair. Xavy, you dropped a mushroom on the floor."

"I did? Oh."

"No, my parents are very worried about us, as well they might be."

"Are *you* worried?"

Susannah finished draining the spinach before she answered. "Not so much now."

"But back in November?"

She began to peel the onions, which made her blink her eyes. She did not answer.

"I suppose that's best forgotten," I said.

She nodded. I helped her with the onions, and soon we were both sniffling.

"Can't I talk about it at all?"

"No," she said, shaking her head solemnly.

"As long as you're over it now," I said.

"I'm over it," she said.

Later, while I was watching everything bubble along on the stove and Susannah was setting the table in the dining room, I thought how strange it was I had been enamored of her for so long. She was not at all my sort of person. We had never been able to talk to each other in a relaxed way. I had always been ill at ease and tense, always watched myself nervously when I was with her, never knew quite what to say. How had I sustained such a groundless infatuation for two and a half years? The whole thing seemed boring and ridiculous to me now.

My book is coming to an end, and I do not have the energy to present a detailed description of yet another ceremony. I did well by the wedding and the funeral, but I will have to slight the christening.

Mr. and Mrs. Twombley had come for several days this time. Timothy Twombley was with them, dutiful and bored. Jeff did his best to find things for him to do, outfitting the Grizzly, but Timothy preferred to saunter about the village putting on his most attractive Appalachian accent for the local girls.

Mrs. Twombley would hardly let her grandson out of her sight. She was always worried he would tip over and kept propping him up and fussing with his clothes. Mr. Twombley, more rotund now and balder, liked to bounce his grandson on his knees and endlessly repeat the rhyme of Humpty-Dumpty to him. They paid little attention to me.

Mrs. Kimberk was an unruffled hostess who managed large elegant meals by unobtrusively drifting into the kitchen now and then. For all Jeff and Susannah had said about her depressed state, I could detect nothing of it. Jeff himself was much happier than he had been the night we stayed up and talked. He was so full of enthusiasm for his venture north, and he tried his hardest to entrance his father-in-law with every possible detail of his plans for surviving in the raw elements.

The two old aunts, Wilsey and Whalen, came out from the city for the christening. They were failing more than they had been at the time of the funeral, but they remembered me well, and we had a lively discussion about the war before we went into the church.

At the font in the spare, stern Episcopal chapel, Susannah held her baby in her arms, looking at him with her green eyes downcast, her long red hair falling about her shoulders. Philip twisted about with wide eyes as the minister stepped forward to perform the rite.

That evening, after another splendid meal and perhaps a surfeit of family, Zada and I felt like taking a walk. Susannah was at the piano in the back parlor playing the E-flat major Chopin prelude, rippling it along with an extremely gentle touch. Jeff was holding Philip and turning pages. The Twombleys and Mrs. Kimberk sat in the front parlor listening. Timothy was trying to find *one* interesting book among all those he had to choose from.

Zada told her mother that she and "Xavier" were going out. Mrs. Kimberk, intent on the music, put her finger to her lips, then looked up at Zada quizzically, perhaps because she had called me Xavier, or perhaps with a certain half-formulated suspicion. We slipped out as quietly as possible.

It was a soft spring evening, the sky was black and clear, and there was no breeze at all. We walked to the lake and talked about the fussy Twombleys and the two dependable old aunts. It was not until we were on the beach itself that we talked about ourselves.

"Want to sit down and get some sand on your bottom?" I said.

"Yes," said Zada. So we sat.

"There's the Great Bear," I said.

"The Big Dipper. Do you call it the Great Bear?"

"No, only when I'm romantically inclined."

I put my arms around her, and we lay back on the sand. I was entirely happy with her, relaxed, almost expansive, not at all constrained.

"What if we do get married someday?" I said. Zada and I had discussed it before.

"What if we do?"

"I'm absolutely sure we will," I said. "We know each other so well."

"But won't you always in the back of your mind think of me as the dumpy little sister?"

"Has that been bothering you? You were never dumpy."

"Horsy, then."

"I won't think of you as the horsy little sister any more than you'll think of me as the cloddy older friend."

"I never thought of you as that."

"What did you think of me as?"

"The person I'd like to marry." She ran the back of her hand along my cheek and down my neck, and I gave her a quick kiss.

"You're just like Jeff as far as predetermination goes," I said. "Why didn't I ever suspect this would happen?"

"Oh, I never suspected it would happen. I just wanted it to. What *did* you think of me as, Xavier?"

"I don't know. I didn't think. You see how stupid I was. But now I think you're the most lovely sight my eyes can see."

"No, you don't," she said.

"Yes, I do!" I wrestled with her and pinned her, giggling, on her back. "Give up?" I tickled her until she said yes, and then we lay still and did not speak for a while.

"Do you have a middle name, Xavier?" Zada said, pulling herself up on an elbow to look down at me with my head on the sand. It was dark enough so we could not see each other very clearly.

"No, I'm just plain X. F."

"My middle name's Elizabeth after my mother and also in case I didn't like having as unusual a name as Zada when I grew up."

"How will Z. K. F. look monogrammed on a towel?" I said.

"Are we going to have monogrammed towels?"

"Hundreds of them."

"Jeff and Susannah gave all theirs away."

"Your brother is a little crazy," I said.

"Yeah, and maybe you're just marrying me for my trust fund."

I wrestled her to the ground once more. "On the contrary, we'll use it to set up an agency in aid of starving vagrants in the North Woods."

"Mean!" said Zada. "Let me up."

We both sat up side by side and could barely see the

wavelets out of the dark sinking into the sand at our feet.

"No," said Zada, "we'll be rich, that's all. Nothing to make apologies for."

We were quiet again, and I came to the conclusion that it *would* be something to make apologies for, given the state of things, so I said, "But we'll live modestly when it comes down to it. Maybe we could buy a little farm and live in a rustic sort of way. But not far from Boston. You could raise horses. You know, I've never seen you on a horse."

"Want to go riding tomorrow at my old stable?"

"Me? I've never been on a horse in my life."

"You could just watch me then, if you wanted to."

"Oh, I could give it a go, I guess."

"Are you serious about having a farm, Xavier? Did I tell you about the girl in my dorm whose sister and brother-in-law found an old farm? Twenty-two thousand dollars for twenty-five acres, with a house and an old stable and a ring. And they make a bit of money boarding horses."

"And I could raise puppies on the side, specialize in Kamchatkan wolfhounds or some such rare breed. Make a fortune."

"And you could write more books," said Zada. "Hey, by the way, when am I going to get to read . . ."

"Soon," I said. "I still have some finishing touches to put on it."

But first I let Dr. Lichty read the manuscript as it ends above. He was horrified when I told him I was going to let Zada read it.

"You're a damned fool!" he said in his gruffest voice. He has heavy black whiskers and a bearish face, but a kindly one even when he is perturbed with me. I had not expected such a response. I tried to explain that Zada and I had promised not to keep anything from each other.

"What makes you think she wants to know all that?" said Lichty. "You've said yourself she's a private person. That's what you like about her. She knows you've had difficulties, she knows your relations with other people have not as yet been very satisfactory. If she's at all sensitive to such things, she's probably aware of your former interest in Susannah. She's content to let it stay where it is. The seamy details don't make any difference."

"But what if they should come out someday?" I said.

"Do you seriously think they will?"

"Even if only hinted at, or suspected. I don't want any suspicion hanging over us, Dr. Lichty." I was convinced of the outrageousness of his position.

"But you will agree that a person who is unsure of himself," said Lichty, pointing one of his pipe cleaners at me, "is likely to spout out the truth rather self-righteously, as if to say, 'Look how honest and free and true I am!' while in reality he's undercutting himself

226

on purpose, exposing his weaknesses, so he'll have to fail once again."

"But won't the book show her how much I love her, and won't she feel tremendously relieved because nothing of the past can ever bother us, it's all in the open?"

"Mr. Fereira, you're dealing with the deepest of feelings. Zada's Jeff's sister. How will she feel reading about him as a cheated-upon husband? Will she carry your truth principle to its logical extreme and tell her brother about his wife's behavior?"

"No," I said.

"Why not?" Lichty said, with a snap of his jaw.

"Because Zada isn't marrying Jeff."

"But surely the responsibility between a brother and a sister . . ."

"I don't understand what you're trying to do, Dr. Lichty." His arguments were very upsetting to me.

"I'm trying to make you aware of what you may be doing to yourself if you let Zada read your book."

"And what if I'm sure it's not self-destructive, if I really believe it will be good for us both in the long run?"

"Do you believe that?"

"Yes."

"And are you prepared to make this girl you've come to love see herself as an awkward adolescent again, and what's worse, through *your* eyes? And see *you* as a victim of your insecurities and perhaps as an opportunist? Isn't there something rather sinister in the story of a guy who commits adultery with his best friend's wife two months after their first child is born and then goes on to win over his sister and with her all the money that used to be his?"

"But you're taking everything out of context!"

"You can't be certain, Mr. Fereira, how the book will affect Zada. She's still a little unsure of herself, I would guess. But is it necessary to take the risk at all? You must learn to be more of a private person yourself, an objective person, not someone who scatters himself all over the place. Do you have to make sure Zada will accept all your past failures before you can be sure she'll grant you any future successes?"

"No," I said.

"Then think about it before you let her read that book. The book was necessary for you, but it's not necessary anymore. You've laid the groundhog, groundwork, I should say."

That was Lichty's prize Freudian slip. We both were highly amused.

"But she wants to read it," I said, serious again.

"She has no idea what's in it. Of course she wants to read it. She loves you and everything you do."

"But what can I tell her?"

"Couldn't you write something else as a substitute, an invented story, with yourself out of it? You might find you have a talent for it."